Wendelin Van Draanen

How I Survived Being a Girl

HarperTrophy®
An Imprint of HarperCollinsPublishers

Special thanks to my husband, Mark Parsons,
for his undying support and enthusiasm,
and to Nancy Siscoe,
who has believed in me from the beginning

HarperTrophy® is a registered trademark of
HarperCollins Publishers Inc.

How I Survived Being a Girl
Copyright © 1997 by Wendelin Van Draanen Parsons

Library of Congress Cataloging-in-Publication Data
Draanen, Wendelin Van.
How I survived being a girl / Wendelin Van Draanen.
    p.   cm.
Summary: Twelve-year-old Carolyn, who has always wished she were a boy, begins to see things
in a new light when her sister is born.
ISBN 0-06-026671-6 — ISBN 0-06-054073-7 (pbk.)
[1. Self-acceptance—Fiction.   2. Brothers and sisters—Fiction.   3. Family life—Fiction.]
I. Title.
PZ7.D779Ho   1997   96-14565
[Fic]—dc20   CIP
                                                                                         AC

Typography by Alison Donalty
❖
First Harper Trophy edition, 1998
Revised Harper Trophy edition, 2003

Visit us on the World Wide Web!

www.harperchildrens.com

*Dedicated with love and gratitude
to my parents, Peter and Mieske Van Draanen
and my siblings, Mark, Arlen, and Nanine*

CONTENTS

SCHOOL

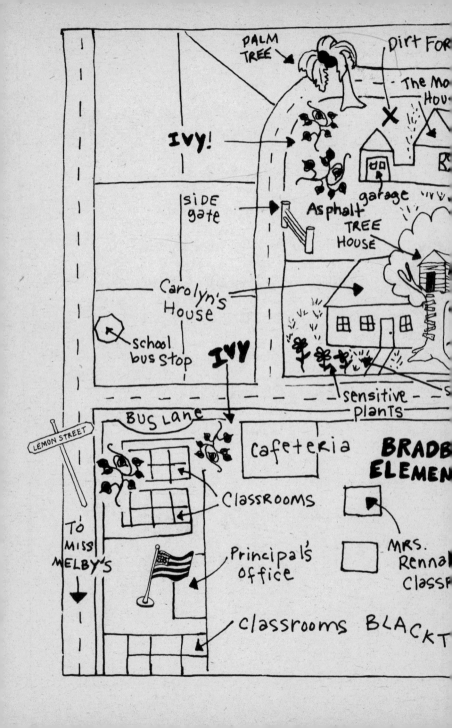

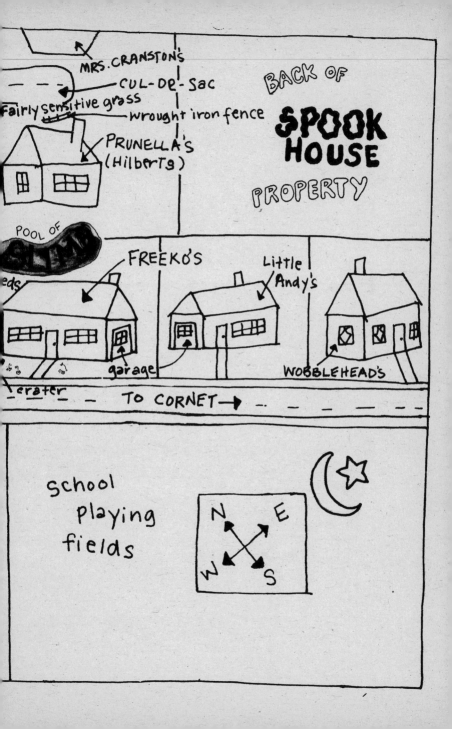

So you See...

Things had been a certain way since I could remember and then all of a sudden they were just different. Anybody else would tell you things were the same as they'd always been, but they weren't.

It happened about the time Nancy came along, and there are probably a lot of people who think she should've come sooner. They say she's the one who tamed me a bit—even made me quit wishing I was a boy.

Course, Charlie might've had something to do with that, too. . . .

SUMMER

chapter 1
The Freekos

Jack and Allen didn't help matters much. Picking on me and all. Just something brothers do, I guess. Call you names. Pound on you. And worst of all, ditch you. Now, it's one thing to get ditched because you're whiny or slow or a big-mouth. It's another thing to get ditched because you're a girl.

Things started looking up, though, when Jack decided he'd ditch Allen too. Billy and the boys were always ditching their little brothers, and Billy being Jack's best friend, well, you know how it is.

So Allen and I started hanging around together more, and one of the things we did a lot of was spying. Spying's great fun. It gets the blood pumping, *ba-boom! ba-boom! ba-boom!*, right up in your ears so you almost can't hear anything else.

Everyone knows that when you go spying, you've got to wear dark clothes, and most people think that's because you want to be able to hide, which is true, but dark clothes also put you in the *mood*, and there's nothing better than being in a spying mood.

One night we tossed our beanies out the window and told Mom we were going across the street to the school to play hide-and-seek with some friends. She said that was just fine without even looking up from her knitting, and Dad was busy wrestling with the wiring of a lamp, so it was no problem slipping by him.

Allen wanted to go clear down to the Spook House, but I convinced him we ought to see what was happening over at the Freekos'.

The Freekos were easy to spy on, and we never felt bad about doing it because they weren't very nice people. They hated us way before we ever *thought* about spying on them.

When I say spying on them was easy, I mean *easy*. Normally we spy on people doing stuff in their yards. We don't go looking in just anyone's windows! But the Freekos didn't have drapes, so you could go right up to the window and peek inside. Now, you may think that's not very nice of us, and you're right, but you have to understand that when you've got neighbors like the Freekos, you find yourself doing stuff you know you shouldn't, and pretty soon you just get carried away.

Anyway, Allen and I peeked in the front windows and then in the kitchen window, but we didn't see anybody, and it's not much fun spying on a sink full of dishes. So we looked over the back fence, and boy did that make our eyes pop open! Freeko was lying on his stomach by the pool in a pair of old underwear and he wasn't moving. Not at all.

Allen looked at me and whispered, "Is he dead?"

Well, he sure looked dead to me, and all I wanted to do was get out of there. I whispered back, "I don't know!" and was just about to say we should leave when Allen started to climb over the fence. I grabbed him and said, "What are you *doing*?"

He looked over his shoulder. "Don't you want to find out if he's dead?"

I didn't want my little brother thinking I was a sissy, so before he could start climbing again, I scrambled over the fence and whispered, "Hurry up!"

We went around the pool over to where Freeko was. Well, it's not a pool like you're used to thinking of. It's got water in it, but you wouldn't want to swim in it unless you were a snake or a frog or something that liked slime.

Anyhow, we got up to Freeko and looked at him for a couple minutes trying to figure out if he was breathing or not. That wasn't easy to do, because he was lying facedown on the cement. I tried to get in close to Freeko's face to see if there was any air going in and out, but all I could really see was his stubbly cheek. Everything else was kind of smashed into the cement, which made me think that maybe he *was* dead, because no one could actually sleep like that.

Then Allen poked him with his foot. Freeko groaned and rolled over, which spooked me so bad I almost fell into the pool. Freeko kind of sputtered and started snoring real loud, his stomach going up and down, up and down, with little rocks from the cement kind of stuck to it.

Allen looked at me and said, "Why's he sleeping out *here*?" but before I could come up with an answer, we heard the sliding glass door open and had to scramble and hide behind a trash can.

Well, Fattabutta came swooping out of the house wearing one of her muumuus. She poked Freeko right in the ribs with her foot and cursed at him something fierce. Freeko mumbled but went right back to sleep, so Fattabutta picked up this booze bottle that was bobbing in the pool and used it to scoop slimy water on him.

Just then we heard Dad calling, "Jack, Carolyn, and Al-len!" which made my heart stop. We couldn't go *any*where with Fattabutta right there.

So we were still watching Fattabutta splashing and cursing and waving the bottle around in the air when it came again, "Jack, Carolyn, and Al-len!"

I grabbed Allen in case he was thinking of making a break for it, and we just watched as Freeko got up on his knees and started crawling toward the house like some kind of gigantic snail. Fattabutta walked behind him, cursing and emptying the bottle on his back.

Just as Freeko was getting up on his feet, we heard, "Carolyn! Allen!" and Dad was sounding pretty mad.

The minute Fattabutta was in the house, we climbed over the fence, popped down into our own backyard, and raced for the back door. I tried to catch my breath and act normal, calling, "We're home!"

Dad was on the verge of being mad, but you could tell he wasn't quite there yet. "Where have you two been? Your mother was getting worried," which is what my dad always says when he's the one who's worried.

I smiled and said, "Sorry! We came as fast as we could."

He frowned a little, but all he said was "Well, it's bedtime."

Allen and I said, *"Already?"* so he wouldn't get suspicious, and then moaned and groaned and headed down to the bathroom to brush our teeth.

We were in the middle of brushing when Jack barged in. Jack always barges in. Even when it's locked. He does this little maneuver with the lock, and *snap*, he's in.

And you could tell something was really bugging him. He put some toothpaste on his brush and said, "Where'd you go?"

Now, I wasn't about to say. He was the one who wanted to go off with Billy instead of us, so let it bug him. But Allen blurted out, "Spying!" I just scrubbed my teeth hoping Allen wouldn't say more, but sure enough he piped up with "We went to—"

So I spit my toothpaste out fast and said, "What's it to you? You didn't want to come with us *sissies*, remember?"

Jack just pretended I wasn't in the room and said to Allen, "So who'd you spy on?"

Allen said, "Freeko! We went back there 'cause we thought he was dead!"

That made Jack quit brushing for a minute. "Dead?"

I couldn't help it. "Yeah! He was just lying out there by the pool, so we decided to kick him to see if he was dead or not."

Jack's eyes bugged out. "You *kicked* him?"

Well, that really got Allen going. He told him all about it, adding a little as he went, if you know what I mean.

Jack looked at us for a minute and said, "I don't believe you," and stood there scrubbing his teeth way more than he needed to.

I knew this was just his way of not having to say anything else, so I said, "What did *you* do tonight?"

Jack scrubbed some more but finally decided he couldn't do that all night. He rinsed his mouth and said, "Nothing," and left. Just like that.

Allen gave me a big grin. "You want to go spying again tomorrow?"

I grinned back and said, "Sure," because it feels

nice, having your brother want to go spying with you.

Then he said, "Do you think Jack'll want to come?"

Well of course I thought he would, but I told Allen that if we really wanted him to come, we'd have to be careful and ask him just right so he *didn't* think we wanted him to come.

Brothers can be complicated that way.

chapter 2
The Moyers

The Freekos are our neighbors on one side, and since we live on the corner we don't have neighbors on the other side. What we do have is neighbors right behind us, and that's the Moyers.

The Moyer family is a lot like ours. They have three kids just like we do: Will is Allen's age—they're in fourth grade—and Charlie and I are both in sixth, but their girl, Mary, is a little bit older than Jack. She's in high school and has never been interested in playing with any of us.

What I know about Mary is that she loves her cat and has a best friend named Laura. When I'm over at the Moyers', I see her around, but usually she and Laura lock themselves up in Mary's room and talk about boys or cats or whatever.

So I was pretty surprised when Will and Charlie came over and told us their sister was going to put on a talent show and that we were invited. Well, I was surprised until I found out it was going to cost me fifty cents to watch. I told them to forget it. Then they told me Mary was going to strip. Now, I couldn't quite believe that, but they promised, and I figured I had to see it for myself.

It didn't take long for the whole neighborhood to be talking about it, and the afternoon of the show these benches Will and Charlie put out in front of their garage door were just crammed full of kids.

Finally the garage door swung open and Laura came out from behind these sheets that they'd nailed to the rafters. She was dressed in this weird suit and black hat and announced that the talent show was about to begin. So we all quit squirming and hushed up. Then Laura and Mary started doing really dumb dances and baton twirls to this record that skipped so much that they had to go over and bump the needle every couple seconds.

This went on for a while, and then someone started booing. Pretty soon a lot of people were booing, and I joined in. I mean, I paid fifty cents to see this show. At our house fifty cents is what you get for picking two big bags of weeds, and I didn't stuff two grocery bags with weeds so I could watch some dumb dances and listen to a skipping record.

All that booing made them stop the record and

whisper for a little while before announcing that it was time for Mary to strip. Of course that made everyone quit booing and start clapping. So they turned the lights in the garage off and some different music came on. Laura stood there, still wearing that stupid black hat, and asked us if we were ready. We all hooted and hollered and clapped, so she pulled back the sheets to uncover this big piece of plywood.

No one wanted to boo yet, just in case, and in a few minutes clothes started coming over the top of the plywood. First shoes and socks, and finally a blouse and a skirt. A couple of the older guys whistled, but I thought it was pretty dumb.

Finally Laura made the big announcement that Mary was naked on the other side and did we want to see? Everyone started hooting and hollering, so Laura announced, "One, two . . . three!" and moved the plywood for about as long as it takes to blink.

Well, they tried to make it quick, but it was easy to tell that Mary was wearing a skin-colored bikini. Charlie and Will brought down the garage door, and everyone started booing their heads off, hollering for their money back.

Of course they didn't give us our money back,

and when they finally got everyone to leave, we said we weren't ever coming back.

Trouble was we liked playing at the Moyers' house because there is always something going on. We play kickball and tag in their backyard a lot, and Mrs. Moyer never complains that we make too much noise like other moms would.

At the Moyers' they're always eating snacks— peanut butter and jelly sandwiches or hot dogs and chips—*good* food. If you go over there in the middle of the afternoon, you can usually find them eating something good and watching baseball.

Lots of times they offer us peanut butter sandwiches, but I always say, "No, thanks." It's more fun to watch them eat. They've got this way of eating sandwiches that's kind of gross, but you just can't help watching them, trying to figure out how the food stays in their mouths. See, they eat with their mouths open. I mean *wide* open. Especially Charlie. He'll take a bite of sandwich and then a swig of milk, and chew. And you can see the bread mixing with the peanut butter and squishing into the milk with little streaks of grape jelly pushing through now and then. And pretty soon it's one big mushy kind of tan paste squishing between his teeth. Then he stops chewing for a minute, swallows, takes a gulp of milk, and starts all over again. It's amazing.

But after a while you get bored with watching, or the sandwich is gone and all there is to do is look at the ball game on television. Allen can stand it longer than I can. I just get antsy and have to leave. Mrs. Moyer always says, "Leaving so soon?" and I always answer, real polite like, "Yeah," and let myself out.

So I guess I was friends with Charlie. I mean, we were in the same grade, and he probably would have invited me to do stuff with him and his friends all the time if it wasn't for the stupid fact that I was a girl. I didn't act like a girl. I didn't even look that much like a girl, because I kept my hair real short and wore boys' clothes any chance I got. It's just that I was a girl, and it made it kind of weird.

Anyhow, a couple of days after Mary's stupid talent show I went over to the Moyers' to find someone to play with, and Charlie had his friend Brent over. Brent lived in a different neighborhood, so he wasn't over all the time like some other kids, but I think Charlie and Brent were best friends.

Since Brent was over, I decided to see what Allen and Will were up to, but Brent called me back to Charlie's room and said, "Hey, Carolyn! Want to see Charlie in his jockeys?"

I was so embarrassed! I mean, Mrs. Moyer was right there in the dining room. Then he did it *again*. "Hey, Carolyn! Come here! This may be your only chance! Charlie's *naked*."

I just stared at Brent and said, "No! I don't want to see!"

He teased me some more and finally I told him to shut up and leave me alone. I mean, what was he thinking? That I've grown up with two brothers and have never seen a naked boy before?

Finally Charlie came out, all dressed, and told Brent to knock it off. He said I could go in his room if I wanted, but I just stood there like an idiot while he ducked into the bathroom to brush his teeth. Then Brent came up to me and said real nah-nah-nah-like, "Everyone knows you've got a crush on him."

That made me really mad. "Do not!"

He just grinned at me like only Brent can grin. It's a real nasty grin, and it made me want to punch his lights out. Instead I said, "Do not!" again, but when Charlie came out of the bathroom, I couldn't stand hanging around, thinking that he thought I had a crush on him. I ran out the door and scraped myself all up climbing over the back fence into our yard.

After that I went straight to my room and stared at my pillow for the longest time. I wished for a friend I could talk to. Like Allen had Will; like Charlie had Brent; like Jack had Billy. And I thought about the girls I knew in the neighborhood and how stupid it was being a girl. And I just stared at my pillowcase until I did what any sensible girl would do.

I cried.

chapter 3
Midgets and Mischief

The Freekos aren't the only ones in the neighbor-hood who are a little strange. It's just that with the Freekos it's obvious. With the Hilberts you have to look a little harder.

The Hilberts live around the corner, right next door to the Moyers, and we never spy on the Hilberts. Their curtains are always drawn, even in the middle of the day, and they have this wrought-iron fence that goes clear around their lot. Most people don't fence in their front yards. Sure, between yards there's some kind of divider, but up along the sidewalk? No one but the Hilberts has that.

I've never seen Mr. Hilbert. I don't even know if there is a Mr. Hilbert. But I've seen Mrs. Hilbert lots. Mostly in her car. She has this big brown car. It has power steering and seats and windows and everything, which she needs because she's so short. She might even be a midget—I don't know. I don't think I've ever seen her just standing. Well, there was the time that her gate was actually open and I went up on a dare to ask if she wanted to buy Girl Scout cookies, which she didn't, but she was real nice about it. She answered the door and she was short all right, but I was down a step so I don't really know if she's a *midget* or not.

So when you see Mrs. Hilbert in her big old car, puttering up the cul-de-sac or back down the cul-de-sac, she always looks straight ahead, clutching the wheel with all her might, concentrating real hard on what she's doing. Mom says she's propped up on a stack of pillows so she can see out the window, and I've always wondered how she reaches the pedals.

Now, Mrs. Hilbert has a daughter, and her daughter goes to Bradbury Elementary just like the rest of us. She's in Allen's class and her name is Prunella, if you can believe that. Prunella Hilbert is not a name I would want for myself. It's bad enough being a girl without having a name like that. Anyhow, Prunella is short and pudgy, and she has one of those noses where the holes are up and out. You know, like a snout. When you look at Prunella, you can see right up her nose almost clear to her brains. If I had a nose like that, I'd worry about it being clean all the time. I don't know what I'd do if I had a cold. Probably stay home a lot.

Prunella isn't someone who comes out to play with the rest of the neighborhood kids. We play kickball at the end of the cul-de-sac, right in front of her house, and she never comes out, even to watch. I can't really picture Prunella playing kick-ball anyway. It can get pretty dusty, and you know what *that* does, even to a regular nose. Besides, I don't think she has any kickball clothes. She's always wearing these lacy dresses and Mary Janes. Shiny black Mary Janes. And she has all this hair. It goes past the middle of her back, all curled in ringlets with a bow somewhere or another. If my mom ever did that to me, I'd take the scissors to it myself! Lucky for me my mom likes my hair short. Sometimes when it's getting kind of long, she'll want to go and curl it, but I always throw a fit, so she winds up cutting it instead.

Long hair's okay, I guess, if you're into dolls. Seems like all girls with long hair play with dolls. Dolls are the most boring thing in the world. Even in the winter. Don't tell anyone, but I tried it once. I got a doll for Christmas from some aunt who didn't know me very well, because she thought I was just "precious." Anyhow, I tried playing with it after I was supposed to be in bed, but let me tell you, it was a waste of time. It wound up under my bed, and it stayed there until my mom came along and made me clean up my room.

I always figured Prunella had dolls—lots of dolls. And while the rest of the neighborhood was out playing kickball, she was probably in her room dressing her dolls and fixing their ribbons. So you can understand why I was pretty surprised one day when she pounded on our door and rang the door-bell nonstop at the same time.

I couldn't understand a word she was saying. Partly it was that nose, all flaring in and out like it was. Partly it was that she was just *babbling*. I wanted to get Mom, but she hadn't been feeling well and was taking a nap, so I wanted to make sure it was an emergency before I woke her up. I said, "Prunella! Stop it! What's the matter?"

She said, "Allen and Will!" and then a bunch of really fast words that I couldn't understand.

"What about them?" I asked, thinking she'd gone nuts.

"The car! They crashed the car!"

I just stared at her for a minute. I mean, it was

awfully warm out and I was thinking that maybe she just needed some lemonade. Finally I asked, "What do you mean? Whose car?"

Up and down jumped Prunella in her Mary Janes. "The Moyers'! Their new one!"

Well, Will's family *had* gotten a new station wagon a few days before, but I still thought she was nuts. "Prunella, what do you mean 'they crashed the car'? How could they crash a car?"

Those Mary Janes were flying. Like someone was turning a jump rope way too fast. She practically screamed, "They just did! They crashed the car. Right into our fence!"

Well, this I had to see. That would be some trick. I mean, Allen and Will were too *short* to crash a car. *I* was too short to crash a car. Then I remembered that Mrs. Hilbert had crashed their car once, so I thought, Well, if someone who was probably a midget crashed a car, then maybe Allen and Will did figure out a way to crash the Moyers' car after all.

I looked at Prunella stomping up and down and decided that she probably wouldn't be wanting any lemonade. I said, "Come on. Let's go," and closed the front door tight.

She came flying after me, squealing, "Wait! I'm supposed to get your mother."

I just hopped down the steps and said, "She isn't home."

"She isn't home? Where *is* she? She *has* to be home!"

I swear she was going to go back and take a look for herself, only I cut right across the front yard and hollered over my shoulder, "Well she's not," so she decided to chase after me instead.

We turned the corner, and from the top of the cul-de-sac I could see the Moyers' brand-new station wagon popped up over the curb with its nose scrunched into the Hilberts' wrought-iron fence. Mrs. Moyer was a little ahead of us, walking down the sidewalk really fast, and Allen and Will were scuffing at the rocks at the edge of the road looking like they'd already been whipped.

When we got down to the wreck, Prunella disappeared inside her house and Mrs. Moyer took Will by the ear and hollered at him a few minutes before spanking him. Right there in front of all the neighbors, *whack!* He didn't cry, but he came pretty close.

I ran up to Allen, who was pretty glad to see me, and whispered, "What *happened?*"

Allen looked sideways at the neighbors and said, "We crashed the car."

I knew that, but I tried to be nice about it and asked, *"How?"*

Allen was just about crying. "I don't know! We got in and started pushing all these buttons. It just started rolling! I tried to steer, but . . ." He looked at the fence lying there on that perfect lawn and just kind of shook his head.

So I said, "We'd better go get Mom," and we were starting up the street when Mrs. Moyer stopped us.

"Carolyn, where's your mother?" She was upset in a big way.

"We're going home to get her. Right now."

She looked at me and kind of raised an eyebrow. "Right away?"

I took Allen by the wrist and started pulling. "Yes, ma'am." Grown-ups always pull you by the wrist when they mean business, and I guess Mrs. Moyer liked the way I was tugging on Allen, because she let us go.

Well, Mom was already up, making herself a pot of tea, but she really looked like she should still be taking a nap. She didn't have any lipstick on and her hair was a mess. She just looked kind of pukey.

I asked her how she was feeling, but I guess I was too polite about it. She gave me one of those looks that grown-ups give you when you haven't said a thing yet but already they don't believe you.

She looked at us sideways while she scooped some tea into the pot. When the kettle started screeching, she poured boiling water into the tea-pot and said, "What have you two done." It wasn't really a question. It was more a statement of fact. Mothers are like that. I don't care how smooth you are, moms know when you've messed up. And this was the biggest mess any of us had ever been in.

I didn't think it was safe telling her while she was pouring boiling water, so I stalled. "Well, it's not that bad, really. . . ."

She put the lid on the teapot and looked at me with one eyebrow popped way up. "Oh?"

"It really was just an accident. . . ." I was think-ing that Allen should be the one telling her, only I was afraid he'd start crying before he got the story out. Then Mom would really be worried!

She moved the teapot over to the dining-room table, and I got her a hot pad to put under it. Allen kind of followed along, shivering like he was cold

or something. Mom said, "What was just an accident?"

She was sitting down and she wasn't pouring
tea yet, so I figured it was time. "You know the
Moyers' new station wagon?"

Mom nodded and then kind of froze, so I
decided to just come out with it. "Well, it was
parked on the street and Allen and Will were
playing in it and it started rolling down the hill
and crashed into the Hilberts' fence."

Her eyes popped right open and she said,
"*What?*" and pulled Allen toward her and started
asking him if he was hurt, real panicky like.

Well, that got Allen crying. Bawling, actually.
So I said, "He's fine, Mom. We walked all the way
home. He's fine. So's Will."

Mom looked at me. "How on earth . . . ?"

"He told me they were just playing around,
pushing buttons, and it started to go."

Mom popped out of her chair and looked pretty
awake all of a sudden. She grabbed us both by the
wrists, and off we went. And when she saw the
Moyers' car, she stopped and stared and then asked
me, "Did you see this happen?"

I shook my head. "Prunella came and told me
about it."

She turned to Allen and said, "How'd you get in the car?" He told her that it wasn't locked and they'd just climbed in. Then she wanted to know who was driving and Allen said *he* was.

Now, Mom can get pretty mad. She's not really that big—actually Jack's catching up to her already—but when she's mad, boy, she sure *seems* big.

And Mom was mad, all right. Really mad. I was feeling pretty sorry for Allen, only something seemed kind of weird. She was being kind of rough with us, dragging us down the street by the wrists and all, but she wasn't acting like she normally did when she was mad.

We went down to the bottom of the cul-de-sac, where Mrs. Moyer was talking with a policeman. All the neighborhood kids were out thinking it was pretty neat that Allen and Will had wrecked the Moyers' car. The neighborhood grown-ups were whispering to each other on the far side of the cul-de-sac, and you could tell they were having a good time.

Well, Mom marched right up to Mrs. Moyer and interrupted. She started carrying on about the car being left unlocked and how Allen could have been killed, and it dawned on me that Allen was going to get out of this without so much as a pat on the fanny. I looked over at him and he looked at me, and we tried to look serious but something kept tugging at the corners of our mouths.

Now, Mom and Mrs. Moyer are pretty good friends, and I didn't like seeing them mad at each other, but it was better than Mom being mad at one of us. The policeman did a pretty good job of calming things down, and then he asked a bunch of questions and wrote down all sorts of stuff. Allen liked him, I could tell, because when we were walking home, he said he wanted to be a policeman when he grew up.

Mom didn't exactly drag us back home, but she did walk pretty fast. And when we got home, she sat and brooded for a while and drank cold tea while we tiptoed around the house. Just when Allen was starting to feel like he wasn't going to get killed, Mom picked up the phone and called Dad.

She was in the kitchen with her back turned, so we could get pretty close without her knowing we were listening. You could tell she wasn't trying to get Allen in trouble, she just wanted someone to talk to.

A little while later Dad came home, and he took Allen and went to the Moyers'. It didn't seem fair that I didn't get to go along, but Dad said I had to stay home. That turned out to be okay, because when Jack came home from Billy's, I got to tell him the whole story. And since Mom wouldn't let him go down the cul-de-sac, Jack got really mad because he wanted to see the wreck and couldn't. It made me feel kind of good. It's not every day I know more about what's going on than Jack does.

It was a long time before Dad and Allen came back, and when they did, they were laughing about something or other, so I guess Mr. Moyer and Dad came to some agreement.

The next day Dad and Allen worked on fixing the Hilberts' fence, and by the time they were done, you could barely tell it had ever been down. Jack and I went down to watch a couple of times. I was hoping Prunella would come out so I could show Jack what I meant about her nose, but I guess she was busy with her dolls.

I asked Allen if he'd been able to figure out if Mrs. Hilbert was a midget or not. He said that Mrs. Hilbert did come out to leave them a tray of lemonade, but he was busy helping Dad mix cement and didn't even see her do it. I would've asked Dad, because he *must* have seen her, but under the circumstances I figured I better not.

chapter 4
Fun in a Foxhole

For a while after they crashed the Moyers' car, Allen and Will didn't play together too much. I think our moms were trying to keep them busy with other stuff. But that didn't last too long, and before you know it everyone seemed to forget about the wreck.

So Allen went back to playing over at the Moyers', but I didn't much feel like it. Not that anyone else ever knew what Brent had said, though Charlie must've.

Charlie's always real polite to me. Of course he's real polite to everyone. That's just the way he is. I think my mom actually doesn't like Charlie that much because he's so polite all the time. Doesn't think it's natural. Anyhow, whenever Charlie sees me, he's nice to me, and that didn't change after stupid Brent made fun of me.

So one day I was in my room, minding my own business. Actually I was in the middle of this great mystery and I could've stayed there all day reading it. But when Allen came in with Will and little Andy, Billy's brother, to ask if I would come even up teams at the Moyers', I didn't have much trouble putting the book down. I mean, when three boys come over and ask you to be part of their team, it makes you feel pretty good.

What I didn't know was that they were having dirt-clod fights. And since Will and Allen wanted to be on the same team, that stuck me with little Andy. I should have told them to forget it and gone back to my mystery, but I didn't want them to think I wasn't any fun. I mean, the next time they might not ask me, right? So I teamed up with little Andy and started hurling dirt-clods.

Now, the Moyers' front yard wasn't in the best shape to begin with. They're on a corner, too, and have this big strip of ivy going around the yard right alongside the sidewalk. I always thought that was a pretty good way to keep people from cutting across their yard. It's *thick* ivy with big dark leaves, and if you want to cut through ivy like that, your screws aren't quite tight. You can never be sure what's waiting for you in thick ivy. Mom says that's where black widow spiders go during the day because it's nice and dark and cool. And it's no secret that snails and slugs get together under those leaves to rest after sliming the neighborhood all night. Follow one of those shiny trails sometime—it'll go straight to an ivy patch.

Anyhow, the Moyers had this ivy that was doing just fine. And they had some bushes along the garage wall—the kind with the real dark leaves and red berries. They were doing fine, too. So were the trees. Well, one was a palm tree, and I don't really know if you'd consider that a tree or not. You can't climb it, and you can't build a tree house in it, and it doesn't give any shade, so if it is a tree, it's not a very good one.

Anyway, all the plants were doing fine except the grass. The grass was completely torn up. With the neighborhood kids coming over all the time, it was doomed. And when we started, it seemed harmless enough to be breaking off dirt-clods and throwing them at each other. It's not like that dirt was going anywhere. We were just shuffling it around some.

Besides, Mrs. Moyer could see us playing in the yard because we could see her, sitting at the dining table, clipping things out of the paper. She never said one word about us tearing up what was left of her grass, so we figured she didn't mind.

The dirt-clod fight wasn't much fun. It's not that I got hit so much, although one got me in the back of the head, then broke up and went down my back and into my shorts. But Allen and Will got dibs on the bushes by the garage, and that left little Andy and me with no protection except for that palm tree. And since the tree was right next to the ivy, we had to step in the ivy once in a while, which was real distracting.

So we threw clods around for a while, but when I tripped on a sprinkler and fell backward into the ivy so that even my head was under the leaves, I'd had it. Little Andy was glad and said he had to go too, and since Allen and Will didn't want to fight each other, that was the end of that.

I wasn't planning to get in another dirt-clod fight the next day. Mom had made me take a bath the night before, and there was no way I was going to take a bath two days in a row. So I was just out for a ride, coasting past the Moyers' on my bike, when *thud!*, a dirt-clod broke up right in front of me. I got off my bike real quick, and what I saw was amazing.

There was a group of boys where little Andy and I had been the day before, only they were in these foxholes with piles of dirt protecting them and stacks of dirt-clods everywhere. Allen and Will and a couple of other guys were where they'd been the day before, only now they were getting their bottoms kicked.

Well, I couldn't just ignore what was going on, so I stood on the sidewalk and watched. When they called a five-minute truce and Allen and Will hollered at me to help them dig another foxhole, what could I say?

So we dug and we dug, and pretty soon we'd forgotten all about the dirt-clod fight and were building forts. *Underground* forts. The foxholes kept getting bigger and bigger, and deeper and deeper, and they were really cool inside. All you had to do was just lie against the wall and you'd cool right off. On top of that they smelled good. They even smelled clean. Now, you may ask how dirt can smell clean, and I don't know how to explain it to you except to tell you to go out in your yard and dig yourself a hole. You'll see what I mean.

Pretty soon everyone wanted their *own* hole. It's just one of those things. It gets crowded in a hole, and pretty soon you want out, but you don't want to leave. What you really want is for everyone else to leave, but they don't, so you start making your own hole.

And that's how we wound up with all these holes. Every day we'd all bring sandwiches and eat lunch in our own little fort, and sometimes we'd throw food back and forth, but mostly we just sat and yelled stupid stuff at each other.

Then one day someone had the idea of connecting the holes. We all thought it was a great idea and started digging like mad again, tunneling to the nearest other hole. It was even more work than digging the hole to begin with, but it was really exciting when you finally connected to the hole next to you. What happens is the dirt starts sounding different, and pretty soon it's sounding hollow. That's when you know you're almost there. Then you jab with your trowel and it just shoots right through, and you hoot and holler and back right out and yell that you made it. And anyone who hasn't quite made it yet just ignores you and starts working twice as hard to finish their tunnel so they can hoot and holler and get ignored too.

I don't really know what Charlie's parents thought of all this. Mr. Moyer came home every day around six. He'd open the side gate and park his car in the garage. Then I guess he'd go straight into the house. I never actually saw him the whole time we were tearing up their yard.

Mrs. Moyer, on the other hand, was home, and you'd see her peeking out every once in a while. I'm sure she knew what was going on, but she never actually came out to see. All I know is that Will and Charlie were right in the middle of the action and loving every minute of it. I think they like having as many friends as they do. They go to other people's houses like everyone else, but I think they like it best when people visit them. And all the people they ever knew had heard about the tunnels and were wanting to come over and play.

Then one day Charlie had some friends over that I'd never met before. They were getting kind of wild, crawling through the tunnels and running *across* the tunnels. Now, I know what you're thinking, and of course you're right, but you have to understand that the last thing I wanted was to sound like a whiny girl telling these people I didn't even know to stop walking across the tunnels.

I saw the whole thing happen from my hole. At first I just thought, "Uh-uh, someone caved in a tunnel"; but when Will started calling for help because Charlie was underground, I was out of my hole in a flash, helping to dig him out.

Now, he was fine. He'd gotten a mouthful of dirt

and was trying to spit it all out while everyone else was pushing clumps of dirt off him. He shook out his hair like a dog shakes water out of its coat, and dirt went flying everywhere. When we knew he really *was* all right, we kind of scuffed around a bit. Then when Charlie went inside, everyone else went home.

After dinner Allen and I decided to ride by the Moyers' to see if anything was going on, and sure enough, Mr. Moyer was out with Charlie, filling in all the holes, trying to get the yard back in order. We got off our bikes and asked if we could help. Mr. Moyer just smiled and said no. He didn't seem to be mad at all, but Mr. Moyer's like that. Always real nice and polite. We said we were sorry about the mess, and he said that it was all right—that he'd been meaning to redo the yard anyway.

Charlie, on the other hand, didn't seem quite himself. I don't think he was hurt or his father wouldn't have been making him fill in holes. He just looked like he wished we'd go away, so we did.

Now, you know how mad I got when Brent said I had a crush on Charlie. And you know he just said it because he's mean, not because there's any *truth* to it. But that night I couldn't go to sleep, thinking about Charlie under all that dirt.

And it bothered me, thinking about it, and thinking about it bothering me bothered me even more. Not that it's not normal to be shook up a bit, seeing one of your friends buried alive—it's *perfectly* normal. And I'd go to my grave swearing it would be a lot worse seeing Jack or Allen pulled out of the dirt like that. But it's not true.

And that's what bothered me so much. If it had happened to Allen or Jack, I would have been upset. But this was a different *kind* of upset, and I couldn't get it to make any sense.

And lying there thinking about it for so long didn't help. It got to the point where I didn't care if I figured it out or not. All I wanted was for it to go away.

chapter 5
The Crater

The Freekos aren't bad people. They're just slobs. And most people probably never noticed that the Freekos' stucco was all cracked and this dirty gray color. What they did notice, because you couldn't exactly *not* notice it, was their yard.

It's not like my parents had the most pristine yard, but at least you didn't walk by and say, "Geez, what a mess," like you did when you walked by the Freekos'. Their yard looked worse than the Moyers' did with all those foxholes.

The weeds came clear up to my shoulder, and in the summer they'd dry up and wave around. That was all right if you were spying, because no one from the sidewalk could see you. But when it came to having to weed our own yard, it was another story.

We were always having to weed our yard. Bags and bags of weeds. Mom and Dad had planted dichondra grass, of all things, and around the edge of the yard they'd planted decorative strawberry plants. These are *sensitive* plants, and every time you turn around, you've got to weed or water or do something to keep them going. Why Mom and Dad didn't plant St. Augustine grass is something I still don't understand. That's what they've got at the park, and it's tough stuff. Walk barefoot on it some-time and you'll see—it's nice and cool and thick. I asked the guy on the riding mower once what kind of grass it was, and he told me St. Augustine, which is how I know.

Anyhow, we were stuck with dichondra that we weren't supposed to walk on, and strawberry plants that were a double waste because they didn't give off any strawberries. They did all right in the shade right by the house, but the part of the yard next to the Freekos' was always in terrible shape. Their weeds would blow over and say, "Wow! This is great! There's *water* over here!" And when there's an army of weeds waving in the wind, tossing seed bombs in your direction, it can be downright scary if you think about all the weeding you're going to have to do.

Dad did try to reason with Freeko. He even offered to keep his yard mowed, but Freeko always said no, that he'd take care of it himself. He never did, though. Not until Jack, Allen, and I made the crater.

It didn't start out as much. Actually we were just going to make a spot to hide little Andy's cat. It was a really stupid cat, or at least we thought so because we liked dogs. I don't remember how cat snitching started, and I don't know why we thought it was so much fun. Usually we'd just take the cat and play with it up in the tree house, then let it go.

Little Andy was onto us about the tree house, though. If we pulled the ladder up so he couldn't get in, he'd stand down there and nag until we were so tired of him, we'd toss him the cat. And then he'd get all mad at us about *that*.

Well, one day Jack, Allen, and I took his cat and put it in a box. We punched lots of holes in the box and gave the cat some water and decided to hide it in the middle of the Freekos' yard.

The trouble was, when we put the box down, the weeds folded over and pushed other weeds down and you could tell something was there. So we started pulling weeds to make a flat spot to put the box while we told each other to hush because we weren't sure whether Freeko and Fattabutta were home or not.

Just when we had everything about set, the bottom broke out of the box. One minute Jack's carrying the cat in the box and the next minute it's streaking off. So we were standing there in Freeko's yard in the middle of the day with an empty box full of holes, and Allen said, "Why don't we make this spot a little bigger and turn it into a grass fort?"

We all started yanking weeds, and once in a while I'd sneak out to the sidewalk to see if you could see the spot, which at first you couldn't. It was great! You could crouch in the grass and hear stuff all around you. First just the grass rubbing against itself; then, if you sat still long enough, you'd hear grasshoppers and see bugs marching all around like you weren't even there.

But after a while it was like being in the car. There just wasn't enough room. Jack started stretching out, pigging up space like he always does. Then I started pushing back, and pretty soon Allen's sniffling that he's getting trampled. So we got up and yanked some more grass. And we got carried away, because before you know it we'd made the crater. You could see it from the sidewalk, and it looked even worse from across the street. In the middle of all these dried-up weeds was this huge patch of black dirt. And let me tell you, it looked really, really stupid.

We were all standing across the street talk-ing about how funny it looked when Freeko and Fattabutta came home. Well, we started walking down the street as fast as we could. Freeko yelled after us but we just ignored him. It wasn't like he was using our names or anything—not the names our parents had given us, anyway.

We made it down to the Spook House and just sat under a tree and waited. Finally, Jack said we should go home through the school's playing fields, so that's what we did, keeping our heads kind of low just in case Freeko could see us over the wall. When we got close enough, Jack looked over the wall at the Freekos' yard, and he started laughing so hard he could barely talk. He gave Allen and me boosts so we could see too. It looked like something from outer space had landed in Freeko's yard.

Well, that night we were eating lemon chicken and potatoes, kind of moving our green beans from one side of the plate to the other. Jack, Allen, and I kept pulling faces at each other, hoping we wouldn't get in trouble about the crater even though Dad *must* have seen it when he got home from work.

Just as those beans were getting to be about the only thing left on my plate, Dad said, "So what'd you kids do today?"

It shouldn't have made me jump like it did. Dad asks us that every day. But the *way* he was asking was kind of too smooth. So I stuffed some of those green beans in my mouth and chewed like I was much too polite to answer with my mouth full.

The trouble was, Jack and Allen did the same thing—got real busy eating food and drinking milk and smiling with their lips together.

Dad gave Mom a funny look and said, "I see our neighbors have had some landscaping done. . . ."

Allen giggled, so Dad looked at him and said, "You know something about that, son?"

Allen straightened right up. "I saw it. I think it looks better."

Dad's eyebrows popped up. "You do, do you?"

Then Jack shot off with "Well, *I* do. It couldn't have looked much worse. You've said so yourself."

Dad sat there real quiet for a minute, which can be worse than him acting mad. Then Mom said real softly, "They came over this afternoon."

Suddenly there was a green bean tickling my throat and it made me choke. Jack ignored me and said, "Freeko and Fattabutta?" which made Mom look stern and say, "Jack!" like she always does when he calls them that.

Turns out Mom promised the Freekos we'd come over the next day and mow their whole yard. We acted like it was a big deal, but we were really thinking that we'd gotten off easy.

You'd think after a close call like that we'd want to stay home and recuperate from almost having gotten in big trouble, but it doesn't work that way. Not in the summer, anyway.

In the summertime, nighttime's the best. You can run around and not get sweaty. And it smells great out. In the daytime you go across the street to play at the school, and the asphalt about burns up your nose. Just try to play on blacktop during the day. First your sneakers melt; then your feet pop all over the place with blisters. And it's hard to play dodge-ball with blisters popping and sneakers melting.

But at night! You can run up and down the street or all over the playground and it's like you're invincible.

Anyway, we were all outside, sitting on the curb, awfully glad we hadn't been grounded, just kind of wondering what time it was. Time is one of those things I let grown-ups take care of. I have a watch, but I'm not sure where it is. I really only want to know how much time I have left before Mom and Dad call me home, and that's not something a watch can tell you anyway.

We'd already been down to the Spook House, clear around to the railroad tracks, and back up to Lemon Street on our bikes, and we were trying to decide where we could still pedal before Dad called.

Then all of a sudden Jack laughed and jumped back on his bike. Well, of course Allen and I jumped on our bikes and chased after him. That is, until we saw what he was going to do.

He took his bike and rode it straight through Freeko's yard. I mean, *zing!* Straight through all those weeds, straight across the crater, and clear over their driveway. And then he did it *again* straight back at us. Well, he kept on doing it until there were about twenty trails going through the Freekos' yard and all these tire tracks across the crater. Allen didn't have any trouble helping Jack out, but I couldn't decide what to do. I mean, we were going to mow their yard in the morning, so what did it matter? But something told me to stay out of it. For once, I didn't just go along.

chapter 6
Filling Up the No-No Box

There is another girl who lives in our neighborhood. Actually, there are a couple of them.

Three houses down is a family with one girl. When I first saw her, I thought she was a grown-up. She wore grown-up clothes and walked like a grown-up. Well, except for her head, but I'll get to that.

You know how grown-ups are. They *watch* where they walk, which is okay, but it slows you down. Most kids don't really walk. It's too slow. They only do it when they're tuckered out or with their parents. If you see a kid out by himself or with a bunch of other kids, he'll be moving along pretty quick. Maybe not full-out running, but quicker than you can figure out if he's skipping or running or hopping or *what*.

One day it finally dawned on me that this girl wasn't a grown-up, because she walked by the house every morning at the same time. And when I finally watched where she was going, sure enough, she went to the high school's bus stop on Lemon Street.

The girl has a name, I'm sure, but I call her
Wobblehead. She has all this hair. I know I said
that about Prunella, but Wobblehead's hair is even
longer. It's real long and straight. No curlicues or
ribbons like Prunella. And it goes way down to the
bottom of her back, which is longer than you might
think because she's pretty tall.

So she has all this hair, and I think she likes the
way it feels, swishing across her back, because
when she walks, she moves her head from side to
side. Like her neck is loose. Kind of like one of
those toy dogs you see in people's car windows,
bobbing back and forth. I'm sure she could fool a lot
of people into thinking she's a grown-up if it wasn't
for that wobbly head of hers.

The other girl who lives in our neighborhood is
little Andy and Billy's older sister, Karen. To me
she's always seemed pretty darn old, but I guess
she's about the same age as Wobblehead. Whenever I see her, she has curlers in her hair. Big prickly
ones everywhere, and then little bobby pins
crossed over, curling up those hairs that come
down in front of your ears. And she wears either
this big puffy yellow robe with house slippers or
cutoffs with thongs and a tie top.

I've always thought she was kind of fat, but you always get the feeling from her that *she* looks just fine and that *you're* just a little runt. Karen isn't very friendly, and she doesn't really count as one of the neighborhood kids, so you see why I left her out before. I don't think I'd ever even seen Karen out in the neighborhood until a few days after Charlie got buried alive, when I saw her talking with Danny.

Danny is Fattabutta's son. Freeko isn't his real dad, and I don't think they get along too well. Anyhow, Danny isn't home much. Except for about a month there when every night he and some friends would practice their guitars in the backyard by the pool. Drove my dad nuts. He hates loud music and doesn't think music with electric guitars is music at all.

The neighborhood kids would hang out, looking over the fence, trying to decide whether they were any good or not. We weren't spying or anything, we just looked. So we'd be watching Danny and his friends, and pretty soon Will and Charlie'd come out and look over their back fence, and then you'd see Billy's and little Andy's heads peeking over, clear across on the other side of the Freekos' backyard.

I don't think Danny minded us watching. Actually, he used to say something to us once in a while, which he never did any other time. Danny and his friends would all laugh a lot, and sometimes it was probably about us, but mostly I think they were just having a good time.

I thought Danny was kind of fat, but I guess Karen didn't think so. You could see this white roll hanging out from under his T-shirt and over the top of his shorts. And you couldn't help staring at it because his belly button was so big. It wasn't big and round like a saucer—it stretched out sideways and it looked like you could lose something in it.

And of course when you see a belly button like that, you can't help but wonder how in the world you'd keep it clean. I mean I get little fuzzies in my belly button or, if I've been doing something like digging foxholes, a little dirt. But there it is—I can see it. And it's real easy to clean out. With a belly button like Danny's you'd have to lie down and hold a mirror above it just to see inside, and then, well, it'd be a big job to clean.

So whenever I saw Danny, all I really saw was his belly button. If he was wearing something to cover it up, I don't know if I'd recognize him right off. But like I said, it didn't seem to bother Karen much. You'd never see her looking over the fence, but you'd see her talking to Danny for hours right in front of the house. She'd lean against a car in the Freekos' driveway and listen to him talk. And she'd always have her hair done real nice and have toe-nail polish on.

Anyhow, Karen'd be talking to Danny there in the driveway, and we'd hide in the bushes and spy on them. They never talked about anything inter-esting, and it was kind of boring to watch them. I kept expecting them to start smooching, but they never did.

And why all this matters is Jack. You see, Jack was kind of stuck in between. He and Billy were in the same class, and that was lucky for him because they got along okay. The trouble was Billy was gone a lot. Don't ask me where to, he just was. So Jack was left kind of pedaling around the neigh-borhood by himself, and I think that's when he really started noticing Wobblehead and Karen. You know what *I* think of them, but I guess they'd look different to you if you were older. I know they looked different to Jack. As a matter of fact, I think he thought Karen was pretty, and once in a while

I'd catch him watching Wobblehead as she walked by. He'd always act like he didn't care, but I think he wished he was more grown up so they'd notice him and then he wouldn't be stuck in the middle.

So I guess that explains why Jack would do something he *knew* was wrong and that would get him in a lot of trouble if he got caught. Which of course he did. I think he was trying to be more grown up than he was and just got carried away.

I can't tell you *exactly* what they did, but I can tell you this: There are some words you're not allowed to say when you're a kid, and really shouldn't be saying when you're a grown-up. You know what they are and I know what they are and we don't actually have to say them to talk about them.

In some houses they say words like that all the time and it doesn't seem to be any big deal. For example, when the Freekos are in a fight and yelling at each other, boy you know you're going to hear some juicy words. The whole *neighborhood's* going to hear them.

But at our house we have to pay for words that most people don't even think are bad words. If I call someone "stupid," it costs me three cents. That doesn't seem like a whole lot, but it adds up. "Dumb" is two cents, "moron" is three cents, "idiot" is three cents—you get the idea. Mom thought it would be nicer if we weren't calling each other names all the time, so she started this thing called the No-No Box, and anytime you call someone a name, it costs you. When you get to swears, the price jumps to a quarter apiece, so in our house there's a price to pay for using words like that.

I don't know what they were thinking, but Billy and Jack decided to rub leaves on the side of the Freekos' house, making this green stain that spelled out a cuss word. And this word would've cost Jack a *dollar* if he'd said it at home.

Yup, that's the one.

Anyhow, they didn't get caught until they were done, and they let *Freeko* of all people catch them. There it was, in green letters two feet high. And Jack was caught with leaves in his hand, putting the finishing touches on a box that went around the word. He couldn't exactly deny that he'd done it, although he tried.

Freeko yelled at Billy and Jack so loud that the whole neighborhood could hear, and it wasn't long before people were everywhere. That included Karen and Wobblehead and some girl friend of Wobblehead's.

So there Jack was, being yelled at in front of the

whole neighborhood, and he was looking kind of small. Like he was actually younger than he was.

Then Dad showed up. Fattabutta called him to come over. Not on the phone, but from her bedroom window. She just opened it up and hollered. And you should've heard some of the language *she* used!

At first Dad didn't believe that Jack had anything to do with it, but that's just part of being a parent, I suppose. Finally Jack mumbled that all *he* had done was put the box around the outside, which of course nobody believed. It might have been true, I don't know, and I guess it doesn't really matter. He and Billy did it together. And they probably thought it was pretty grown up until all the real grown-ups started yelling at them. Then they probably felt pretty stupid. I mean, it's pretty embarrassing just being yelled at, but in front of all those people?

They tried to scrub it off, but it was stained pretty good. So Dad took Jack down to the store and they bought some gray paint, and the next day Jack painted the whole wall twice.

I don't know what happened to Billy or why he wasn't out there helping. I do know that Danny and Karen were standing in the driveway the whole time Jack was sweating away on that wall, and that they laughed and talked and treated him like a little kid.

Which I wish he didn't think was so awfully terrible. Being a kid, that is. After all, he ought to be glad—at least he's not a girl.

chapter 7
Pebbles Down the Chimney

You're probably thinking we left the Freekos alone after we got caught making the crater and after Jack decorated the side of their house like he did. And for a while we did. But then their weeds started coming back up, and it seemed like every day Fattabutta spent the whole afternoon hollering at Freeko. Fattabutta would go out in the car once in a while, and when she did, Freeko would sit out in the backyard smoking and drinking straight out of a bottle.

One day Will, Allen, and I were up in the tree house trying to figure out who to spy on when Fattabutta came storming out of her house throwing curses over her shoulder at Freeko. Well, we all kind of looked at each other and knew.

We decided to try spying on Freeko from up on his roof. We all dared each other to do it, and before we knew it, there we were in broad daylight, pushing and pulling each other onto Freeko's roof. Once we were up, we kind of crouched and told each other "Sssh!" a lot, but that was pretty stupid because anyone walking by could just look up and there we were.

We worked our way down the back side of the roof on our fannies so we could see Freeko's back-yard, because we thought we might have a great view of him smoking and drinking straight from the bottle.

Turned out he wasn't there, so we just sat there awhile, trying to decide what to do. Then, in the middle of deciding, we heard, "Jack, Carolyn, and Al-len!"

I looked at Allen. "What *time* is it?" Like he's going to know when he doesn't have a watch on either.

He shook his head and started walking *crunch, crunch, crunch* to the edge of the roof.

"Jack, Carolyn, and Al-len!"

I stood up too, and started looking for a way down, but all there was to land on in Freeko's back-yard was cement. So I followed Allen over to the side of the roof, *crunch, crunch, crunch*, and did what he was doing—looked down.

Now, that's a scary thing, being on someone else's roof with your dad calling you, and not knowing how to get down. But when we heard it again, "Carolyn, Al-len!" we knew we had to do something.

So *crunch, crunch, crunch* we went to the front of the house and finally wound up just jumping off the stupid roof into all those weeds.

We raced to our front door and tried to look real calm, and when Dad came back from checking the Moyers', we acted like we'd been there all along.

Dad *was* home early, and he was acting funny. He told us that he was going to make dinner and asked us to set the table real nice and maybe even use a tablecloth. Said he wanted to surprise Mom.

I don't know where Mom was. I thought she was in the house, but I didn't want to go find out because Dad was acting like something special was going on. I kept trying to remember what I had forgotten. I knew it wasn't their anniversary—Mom helps us keep real good track of that—and I knew it wasn't her birthday.

So I got out a tablecloth and I was setting the table, kind of throwing looks back and forth to Allen, when Jack came out from his room looking grumpy. At first I thought he'd gotten in trouble, but Dad was being nice to him, asking him to peel some potatoes instead of making him help with the table.

So when we had the table set, I went over to help Jack with the potatoes because he was being so slow about it. Also, I figured he was grumpy because he knew something I didn't.

Well, that wasn't the reason he was grumpy at all. He whispered, "I saw you guys on Freeko's roof."

I stopped peeling and looked at him, trying to figure out how much trouble I'd be in if he told. "You did?"

"Yeah. What were you doing up there?"

I shrugged, "Nothing."

He snickered. "Boy, are you going to get it if Dad finds out."

I froze. "Are you going to tell?"

He looked at me like I was brain damaged, so I started peeling potatoes again real fast while he worked at getting this one potato perfect. Finally he said, "Wonder what would happen if you shone a flashlight down the chimney."

I looked at him. "A flashlight?"

He kept working on that potato. "Sure." I looked

at him like *he* was stupid, and finally he said, "At night, dummy."

Well now, that was a thought. And it was one I couldn't stop thinking about. I also thought about other things you could do on the roof. Like make scary noises down the chimney so they'd think it was a ghost or something. Pretty soon I was think-ing that we'd really missed out, just sitting up there on the roof.

Dinner turned out nice, and Mom *was* in the house. At first I thought she wasn't feeling well, because the whole time we were making dinner, Dad was telling us to be real quiet; but when Dad went to get her, she seemed fine. She ate all her dinner, too. I kept looking at Allen and Jack, trying to figure it out, but none of us could. So we just ate and tried not to lie too much when Dad asked us what we'd done all day.

After dinner Mom went into the living room and turned on her favorite record. We did the dishes and came up with a plan to go back on the Freekos' roof. The problem was that Dad had told us that he wanted us to stay home while he went to the store to get some things, and we knew if he found out, we'd be in big *big* trouble.

But you have to understand that we'd been talking about this for *hours* and we were all worked up to go. So we went down to my room and set up the Monopoly board and made it look like we were in the middle of a game. Then we changed into our spying clothes and climbed out the window.

This may sound risky to you, but we really thought we'd only be gone a little while. We figured the minute Dad came driving up, we'd jump off the roof and be in the house before anyone knew we were gone.

So we tiptoed out to the side of the house and then pushed and pulled each other up onto the roof. Jack was the one with the flashlight, and he led the way, crunching right across the roof to the chimney.

It doesn't look like it from the street, but the top of the chimney is pretty high. We couldn't see inside at all, which was pretty disappointing, so we wound up tossing pebbles down the chimney.

At first we did just one, but Allen didn't hear it go down, so we tossed another one. You know the kind of pebbles I'm talking about—all roofs have them. Kind of gray and black and smooth.

Then we all decided we wanted to throw our *own* pebbles down, and before you know it, lots and lots of pebbles were going down that chimney. We would've kept right on going, too, but Fattabutta started screaming up the chimney at us.

She was up to about three *dollars'* worth when Dad came driving down the street. We hunched over real quick and went crunching across the roof and got back home as fast as we could.

So we were in my room, barely out of our spying clothes, when Dad came looking for us. We smiled and acted like we'd been playing Monopoly, and he said, "Your mother and I are calling a family meeting in the living room."

We'd never had an official family meeting before. Usually when Mom and Dad want to talk to us, they just talk to us. None of this official business. I was thinking we were in trouble, but Dad wasn't acting mad. He was acting really nice. So we all looked at each other and raised our eyebrows and followed Dad into the living room.

Now, usually your parents are just your parents. You don't really pay much attention to the way they act or the way they look because you're used to them. And if they change, well, you see them every day, so you don't really notice.

Like Dad—he's always been real tall and skinny

and I never even noticed that he was going bald until Will said something about it. It's not like I don't know what my dad looks like, it's just that I see him every day and I didn't really pay attention to the hairs when they fell out one by one. Sure, all those hairs add up, but the point is I didn't really notice.

So you'd think I'd have noticed, but now maybe you won't think I'm so stupid for *not* noticing. We were all in the living room, feeling kind of weird for having an official family meeting, and Mom was just sitting over in her chair with a cup of tea on her lap. Then all of a sudden something happened and she spilled tea all over herself.

Dad rushed over and asked if she was hurt, but she just laughed and said that it was barely warm and didn't hurt a bit. Dad helped her clean up the tea, and then he cleared his throat and asked, "How would the three of you feel about getting a new brother or sister?"

We didn't say much. We just stared. And all of a sudden Mom looked like someone I hadn't seen in a few years. She looked real *different*.

Mom said, "Carolyn?" because I guess my eyes were bugged out, staring at her stomach.

I stuttered, "A baby?" and all of a sudden I started to cry. It's the weirdest thing in the world, but that's what I did. Mom put her arms out like good moms do, and I got a hug. She stroked my hair and said, "I thought you'd be happy."

Well, I *was*, even though I was crying, and I told her so.

She smiled and looked relieved. Then Dad said, "Now kids, I'm really counting on you to help your mother out. Things are going to be a little rough on her for a while, and I want you to give her a hand as much as you can and do your chores without her having to beg you to."

We all nodded and said sure we would, and then the doorbell rang. We looked at each other like "who could that be?" thinking it was too late for Will or Billy to be coming over. Dad said, "I'll get it," and a few minutes later he came back into the living room with a policeman.

You may think from the things I've told you that policemen would be at our house all the time, but it's not true. This was the first time a policeman had been in our house, and at first I didn't know what he was doing there.

Then it hit me. I tried to keep a straight face and

not give us away, but I was thinking over and over, "I'm dead. No doubt about it—I'm dead."

So I was really surprised when my dad said, "See, they're right here."

We started smiling a little bit. Not too much, just enough to look like we hadn't done anything wrong. The policeman squatted down and said to us, "You haven't been outside tonight?"

We opened our eyes wide and said, "No sir. We were playing Monopoly in our room."

Dad nodded. "I can show you if you'd like."

The policeman smiled and roughed up Allen's hair a bit. "No, that's quite all right. I'm sure they just got the wrong kids."

So Dad showed him to the door, and when he came back, Mom said, "What was all that about?"

"Oh, nothing. The neighbors complained that some kids were up on their roof tossing rocks down the chimney." Then he mumbled, "Probably just soused again."

Dad wound up the family meeting, but the whole time Mom looked at us with one eyebrow up just a little. We went back to my room and were in the middle of counting our lucky stars when Mom came in and closed the door behind her. We all froze. She said, "Monopoly, huh?" and walked straight to the window and closed it tight.

We looked at her and she looked back at us. There was no doubt about it, she *knew*. I was thinking, "I'm dead. This time I'm really dead." But what she did next is the most amazing thing I've ever known my mother to do. She said, "I hope you heard what your father had to say. I need your help and I need you to stay out of trouble." She saw our beanies on the floor by the bed and picked them up. "Do we have a deal? Or would you like your father to find out about this?"

We all stared, stunned that she was black-mailing us. Then we kind of nodded and told her sure, we had a deal.

She just smiled—a real pretty smile—and closed the door tight behind her.

chapter 8
Bunk Beds and Batteries

After I found out that Mom was going to have a baby, I really did try to stay out of trouble. I helped her more with chores and tried to keep Jack and Allen from being too loud when she was trying to take a nap. I even tried going to bed when she said it was time.

Actually, I didn't hate going to bed quite so much after we got bunk beds. Allen and Jack used to have them in Jack's room until a few weeks after we found out about the baby and Jack decided he wanted a room to himself. I said it was fine for Allen to share my room as long as we got the bunk beds and I got the top bunk.

That was fine with Jack, and it was fine with Allen, too. He liked the bottom bunk, and there *is* lots to be said for sleeping down there. For one thing, you can make it into a terrific fort. All you have to do is take one of your blankets and push it under the edge of the top bunk mattress and let it hang down.

Another good thing about the bottom bunk is that if you're mad at the guy in the top bunk, you can push your feet up and bounce them around some. They can't exactly ignore you, because they're flopping around pretty good, and they can't get you back. All they can do is hang over and holler at you to stop, or try to catch one of your toes in a spring. Pretty much they just have to wait for you to quit.

So the bottom bunk is pretty good, but the top bunk is where I want to be every night before I fall asleep. Maybe it's just my imagination, but if you sleep on the top bunk, you have better dreams. When you're up off the ground and the moon's peeking through the window, not real bright—just enough to light up the walls a little—all of a sudden it feels like you're in a secret fort way away from anything that's ever bothered you. And when you feel like that right before you fall asleep, you have the best dreams. Sometimes you barely remember them, but they stick with you the whole day, making you smile for no reason.

I've tried telling people about my dreams, but it's not a smart thing to do. Mom is always polite, but you can tell—to her it's just some mixed-up story.

And then I feel kind of stupid for being so excited about it.

So the secret to good dreams is to not tell anyone about them. You can tell them about nightmares or funny dreams, but when it comes to dreams like you get when you sleep on the top bunk, well, *don't*.

Some nights it's time for bed and you're just not ready. You may be tired, but that doesn't have much to do with it. You're just not ready, and that's when it's important to have a really good flashlight.

You may think I'd use a flashlight for spying, but I don't. Flashlights give you away and get *in* the way. Flashlights are for reading. Of course they're also good for putting in your mouth and puffing up your cheeks and lighting yourself up with, but mostly they're for reading.

And when it's time for bed and you just don't feel ready, and your mom's come in three times to tell you to quit giggling, and she's finally sent in your dad to tell you the same thing, that's when you need a good flashlight. There's nothing worse than being in the middle of a really good part of a book and having your flashlight turn that yellow color. Pretty soon it's brown, and everyone knows brown's just a step away from black.

Ever since Dad told us that Mom was having a baby, we were going to bed before we were ready, so my flashlight was going yellow and I was all out of books. Good books, anyway. When I asked Mom if she could take us to the library, she said she wasn't feeling well and I could tell it wasn't a good time to ask about new batteries. I guess that's why I did what I did. I didn't plan it or anything— it just kind of happened.

One afternoon we were riding around, not going anywhere, when Jack said we ought to go down to the Cornet. Well, that sounded like an adventure. The Cornet's this dime store clear past the railroad tracks, down near where they're putting in the new freeway, and I'd never been to the Cornet except in a car. When I told Jack, he laughed and said that he'd been there lots of times on a bike and that it really wasn't far at all.

So off we went, Allen and I pedaling like mad to keep up with Jack. It was fun, screaming down the street on our bikes with all that wind rushing over us. And it *was* easy. No standing up to pedal, no burn in the legs, just moving your feet as fast as you could before the pedals didn't grab anymore.

Then, before you know it, there we were, at the

Cornet. We walked inside and it hit me. I'd never been shopping without Mom or Dad before. Never. That may not seem like a big deal to you, but it was to me, and I think to Allen too. Jack took off, heading for some corner of the store away from us, but Allen and I just stood in the entrance right under the air conditioning vent, feeling the buzz of the fluorescent lights, and all of a sudden we realized— we could do anything we wanted!

What we did was run. We ran from one end of the store to the other, stopping here and there, saying, "Lookit! Lookit!" and going mad finding stuff we didn't even know existed.

Finally we wound up in the toy department, and that's where we stayed. We looked at everything and played with anything that wasn't in a box, and argued over what would be better to get for Christmas.

After we'd been there awhile, I noticed Jack. He was over by the books looking through a *Mad* magazine kind of grinning that grin of his. I got up off the floor because I wanted to see what kind of comics they had, but when I got close to Jack, he said, "What d'ya want?" without even looking up.

So I moved over to look at the books, and the

minute I saw they had some mysteries, my heart started to pound a little.

I mean the books at the library are fine books, but it feels like I've read *all* of them. These books looked great. And I'd never seen any of them before in my life.

I didn't know what to do. I picked one up and read the cover. Then I picked up another and read some out of the middle. Pretty soon I had all these books I wanted, but no money.

No money and no mom. I looked at the prices and found the cheapest one and stared at Jack. I thought about asking him for some money, but you know how Jack is, so I wound up *not* asking him. What I did instead was take a quick look around and tuck that little book under my T-shirt and inside the elastic of my shorts.

I put the rest of the books away and straightened them out, but my hands were shaking and I was worried that someone had seen. Finally I backed away and looked around, and it felt real funny, this book in my pants.

Then I heard "Carolyn!" and I about died. I mean I just knew—I was going to jail. Then I heard, "Allen!" which made me wonder what *he* was slipping inside the elastic of *his* shorts. My mind was going crazy. See, his voice didn't sound right. Nothing sounded right—like everything was underwater. Everything except those fluorescent lights buzzing away. They were really loud.

Maybe he was just trying to sound older, I don't know, but when I realized it was Jack calling us, I was so relieved, I could've cried.

He looked at me kind of mean and said through his teeth, "Let's go," and then started walking to a checkout counter. I followed him, but by the time I got to the check stand, my stomach was feeling funny and my knees weren't holding my legs together too well. Jack put the magazine on the counter and paid for it, and the lady smiled and thanked us for coming, and before you know it, we were walking under that big air conditioning vent and out into the burning sun.

I didn't wait around for someone to take me away to jail. I got on my bike and pedaled to the stoplight as fast as I could. Once we were across the street, my knees quit shaking and all of a sudden I felt great! That lasted until I was about halfway home. The book was cutting into me like crazy, and I hadn't realized it on the way to the Cornet, but it had been so easy getting there because it was all downhill.

So going home was no fun at all. I didn't even like bumping over the railroad tracks. It was hot and my legs were burning from all that uphill, and I was last in line with this book cutting me up.

I could have taken it out and moved it, I suppose, but I was really afraid that Jack or Allen would see me, so I just left it there. When we finally got home and I was safe in my room, I took the book out, and it was all wet from sweat and curled at the corners. I looked at the cover a few minutes and tried to dry it off, but when Mom called me, I shoved it under my pillow and went to see what she wanted.

And what's funny is I didn't want to go to my room to read it. I helped Mom all afternoon and made dinner almost all by myself and just stayed away from it.

But that night when it was time to go to bed, there was my new book, kind of wrinkled and smelling not at all the way a book should, waiting for me.

After a while I pulled it out and started reading it, but I couldn't concentrate. Now, it wasn't the book—it was a good book. And it wasn't the batteries—they were yellow, but not *that* yellow. I just kept thinking about standing in line at the store and the way the checkout lady had smiled at me so sweetly, and I just couldn't read it.

Finally, after Allen was sound asleep, I crawled out of bed and put the book on my bookshelf in between a bunch of other books where no one would ever notice it. Then I tried to go to sleep.

But I couldn't. I tried not to look at the bookshelf, but somehow I always wound up staring at it, and no matter which way I turned, I could hear it calling, "Carolyn ... oh, Carolyn." I swear, I didn't sleep at all that night. Or the next. And the third night I had the most terrible dreams.

I thought about throwing the book out, but that seemed wrong. Here I'd stolen it and I hadn't even read it. Besides, Mom would probably see it in the trash and ask me about it, and then what was I going to do? I thought about giving it to the library, but how was I going to do that without Mom noticing? Besides, all the books I'd ever checked out had hard covers and a plastic wrap over them. They would know right off—someone was trying to get rid of a stolen book.

By the fourth day I couldn't stand it anymore. I took the book, put it in a bag, and got on my bike. I pedaled to the Cornet and went inside to the checkout counter. I put the bag on the counter and said, "This is yours," and left before they could throw me in jail.

I pedaled like mad all the way up the hill, looking over my shoulder the whole time for a police car to come tearing up to take me away.

When I got to the railroad tracks, I stopped and looked back down the hill, trying to get my legs to quit shaking and get my breathing back to normal. Finally I headed home, kind of slow, and by the time I was parking my bike in the garage, I was thinking that maybe Mom would be in the mood to take me to the library, and that she might even stop on the way home to get some new batteries.

chapter 9
Rodents and Reptiles

It seemed like everyone in the neighborhood had a dog. Everyone but us.

Even the Moyers. Theirs just showed up at their door one day, and boy was it cute. Charlie named him Jinx, and Jinx used to sleep on his bed and follow him all around the house. I thought it was really neat, him having a dog. I also liked Jinx because Jinx liked me, and whenever I'd go over to the Moyers', he'd jump in my lap and give me kisses.

Now, you may think that a dog's a pretty normal thing for a kid to have, and you're right. It is. But Mom was worried about us taking responsibility for a dog. "Responsibility" is one of those words my mom says like she's sure you don't quite understand the definition, even though you swear to her that you do.

Mom didn't start saying no to getting a dog just because she was going to have a baby. She'd been saying no for a long time. We had a goldfish for a while, but we'd forget to feed it. Then one day

Mom found it floating on its side and told us we couldn't have another pet until we learned about responsibility.

But after a few months we got up the nerve to ask for another pet. We started out asking for a dog and wound up begging her for a lizard. At first Mom said no. But then we came up with the idea of using the old fish tank lined with some of this orange sand Mom had made Dad haul from the desert. As soon as we mentioned the sand, Mom started thinking a lizard might be okay after all.

The sand really was very pretty, but Dad was tired of it leaking all over the garage. Not that it was making that big of a mess—I think it just reminded him of getting a flat while he was getting us lost in the desert. Most moms bring home jewelry or key chains or something from their vacations. My mom brings home rocks. Or sand. Or pine cones. Dad doesn't really say much, especially if it's something she's found while he's fixing a flat in the middle of nowhere.

Anyway, Mom kept telling Dad she was going to find a use for the sand, so when we thought of a lizard, she shoveled that sand right into the old fish tank, and the lizard house was set up in no time.

The problem was keeping the lizard fed. Lizards like flies, and they don't seem to like much else. They don't like dead flies, either, and you can't just go down to the pet shop and say, "I'd like three dozen flies, please."

We were responsible for a little while, but it wasn't long before we were fighting about who had to go out and catch the lizard some flies. Then one day when we were all roller-skating over at Bradbury Elementary, we heard Mom hollering.

Of course the lizard was dead and Mom was mad at us for weeks, and it took us a long, long time to get up the nerve to try asking for a puppy again.

When we did ask about getting a puppy, she brought up the lizard, and when she was done with that, she started about the goldfish, and we just stood there not saying much.

But every time we brought it up, she'd spend less time talking about the fish and the lizard and start demanding to know who was going to feed the "animal" and take responsibility. Well, it took a long time, but finally one day she said it was okay for us to get another pet.

We didn't know she was talking about a guinea pig. I don't think *she* knew she was talking about a

guinea pig until she read in the paper about someone giving them away. That afternoon she went out
and came back with this thing that looked like a
cross between a rat and a gopher. She told us his
name was Scamper and that he was our new pet.

Great. A guinea pig. But before you know it,
Dad built a cage for it in a corner of the backyard
and it was all moved in. You couldn't take it out to
play because it would run away and you'd have to
spend the rest of the day trying to corner it. And it
didn't learn tricks. We tried, but it wouldn't do a
thing. Not even sit. The only thing it would do is
squeak. And boy, could it squeak! Not like a mouse,
more like a little pig—which I guess is why it's
called what it's called.

Mom decided Scamper needed a friend, so she
went out and came back with *another* guinea pig and
told us her name was Scooter. And she was right.
That shut Scamper right up. He liked Scooter just
fine. It was Scooter who hated Scamper. She'd bite
him and kick him and run like mad to get away from
him, but before you know it we had a cage full of
baby guinea pigs.

All of *them* learned to squeak in a hurry, too. It
didn't take long before there were even more of

them and Dad had to build another cage–one for the boys and one for the girls. And all those guinea pigs spent the day squeaking and eating and messing up their cages, and pretty soon we were fighting about who had to clean the cages. After a while Mom said she was tired of begging us to take care of them and packed them all up and took them to a pet store.

So anytime we even thought about asking for a dog, Mom would give us that Remember-the-fish-and-the-lizard-and-the-guinea-pigs? look and we'd know it was hopeless.

So just when I was thinking we'd never get a dog, Jack got real mad and told Mom he didn't want fish or lizards or guinea pigs—or rabbits or snakes or cats or goats for that matter. He wanted a *dog*. A dog's what a boy's supposed to have, and no other animal would make up for not having a dog. Except maybe a monkey, if she wanted to give him that.

It seemed pretty dangerous, Jack talking like that when Mom was in the middle of starting a roast. But Mom just threw that piece of meat around in this big orange kettle, singeing one side for a few minutes, then another. And it spattered and popped and acted like it was going to explode, but Mom calmly threw it around not saying much of anything.

Allen and I were watching from the corner of the dining room, lying low. Then Jack did something I'd never seen him do before. He waited. He didn't run off mad or say anything else. He just waited. And when Mom was finally done wrestling with the roast, she didn't say a word about responsibility. She just looked at Jack and said, "I'll talk it over with your father."

Jack couldn't believe it, and when Mom asked him to set the table, well, I've never seen him do it so fast in my life. He even remembered to put out the salt and pepper and then volunteered to help Mom with the potatoes.

All through dinner we were pretty quiet, and Dad knew something was up, but he didn't ask. When dinner was over and we were cleaning up, Mom took Dad into the living room, and before you know it Dad was telling Jack he'd take him to get a puppy in the morning. Allen and I had a fit because we wanted to go too, but Dad said no, it'd be a family dog, but he'd only take Jack.

So the next day Jack and Dad went to the pound and came back with this cute little puppy that Mom named Kocory.

That's how we finally got a dog, and he's been great. He's soft and furry and lets you use him for a pillow if you feel like taking a nap in the backyard, and he doesn't squeak or run away, and you don't have to catch him flies.

And he's the one who gave me the idea of trying to touch the moon.

chapter 10
Touching the Moon

Touching the moon was a secret for the longest time, and it's not something I'd tell just anybody about. But since it's not a secret anymore and I officially know that it can't be done, I guess it's okay to try to explain it.

See, Kocory loves to howl at the moon. And I thought him howling at the moon was really neat, so sometimes I'd go out and try to get him going. I'd get down on the grass and start howling like a dog, and pretty soon he'd be howling away, too.

One night it was so hot out that you had the choice of being miserable indoors or being miserable outdoors. I'll take being miserable outdoors anytime. People are just nicer to each other when they're miserable outdoors.

So I was out in the backyard with Kocory, lying on the grass looking up at the sky. It was so beautiful out. Kind of like when you're camping and everyone else is asleep and you can see out your tent and there it is—the *sky*. It's all glittery, and if you look at it long enough, you feel like you're one of the stars.

It's not something you talk about. It's kind of a secret between you and the stars. People may say, "Wasn't it beautiful out last night?" or "Did you see the stars last night?" or something like that. But no one'll ever mention the magic.

So that night I was out in the backyard with Kocory, feeling like one of the stars, when I noticed the moon. It was just a little crescent moon, but that night, lying there looking up, I thought it was the most beautiful thing I'd ever seen. Partly because of the stars all around it, but also because it was so white and thin. And for some reason I stretched my arm way out and put my finger up and tried to touch it.

If I held my finger just right and looked just above the tip of it instead of right at the moon, it really looked like I was touching it, and it felt like it, too.

It's not like feeling the grass or a piece of wood. It's like feeling rain when you're inside, nice and warm and dry. Or like music. You can't really touch music, but think about your favorite song. Boy, can you *feel* it.

And that's what touching the moon's like. Only better. It tingles right down your arm to your spine and makes you want to stay there all night.

I probably would've, except Kocory got tired of being used as a pillow, and then Mom came out and asked me what I was doing. At first I said, "Nothing," but when she sat next to me on the grass, I decided to tell her.

And that was a mistake. I didn't tell her the way I told you. What I said was "I'm touching the moon."

Mom got this look that moms get when they're all panicked but they're trying to stay calm, and she said, "You're touching the moon?"

I just smiled and nodded. Well, she reached over and felt my forehead and asked me if I was feeling all right, and it hit me how stupid I sounded. Touching the moon. Right.

And I didn't want to explain it, and I didn't want to show her how. I didn't want anything but to take my secret back.

But that's the problem with secrets. Ones you have with yourself or ones you have with the stars. The minute you tell anyone about them, the magic disappears. Even as you hear yourself say it, *poof!*, there it goes. No more magic.

And even when I explain it right, it doesn't *feel* the same. Somewhere there's this little doubt that takes over and makes you not even believe yourself. Pretty soon you think there really isn't any such thing as magic.

Pretty soon you're all grown up.

chapter 11
Picking Weeds and Porching Papers

For a while I didn't care about having a job and earning money. It was always the older kids in the neighborhood who got the jobs anyway, and if you wanted some extra money, you had to make a deal with your mom and dad to get it. Unless you were Mary Moyer and decided to make some money by putting on a stupid talent show.

Anyway, one day Allen and I were standing in the wading pool, cool all the way up to our ankles, when we saw Charlie and Will working their way up the cul-de-sac, knocking on doors. Turns out they were asking everyone if they could wash their cars for a dollar. That got me thinking that if Charlie and Will were old enough to make money from the neighbors, then I was, too.

The trouble was being a girl; people don't think to give you a job they've been wanting a *boy* to do, so I wound up begging Mom for extra work, and all she could come up with was picking more weeds.

So I picked weeds for*ever*—sacks and sacks of

them. And when allowance time came, Jack saw my extra money and it really bothered him. That's when he decided to get a paper route.

I thought it was great fun, him having a paper route. Every day this man would come and drop off a big stack of papers, which Jack would have to fold before he could deliver. At first he wouldn't let us touch even one of his papers, but after a while he got tired of folding them and didn't mind that Allen and I wanted to help.

We folded them all up into themselves so that they made this neat little square that you could just fling. Underhand, overhand, sidearm—any way you tossed it, *zing!* It would slice right through the air.

Allen and I used to follow Jack as he tossed those papers all over the neighborhood. At first he didn't want us going with him, but after a while I think he liked having us around, because he would ask us if we were ready to go, and the three of us would pedal around together.

It was about this time that Mrs. Cranston asked Dad if Jack would want a job doing her yards once a week. Well, Jack didn't want the job. He was too busy making money as a paper boy. So I shot up with "I do!" which Dad thought about for a minute and said, "Why not?"

He took me to meet Mrs. Cranston, who I already knew, but I guess she didn't know me. Funny how grown-ups are about that. I mean, all the kids in the neighborhood know all the grown-ups. If you saw one go driving by, you could say, "There goes Mr. Kingston," or "Look! Mrs. Holt has a new car!" I mean, you just know them, whether they have kids or not.

Grown-ups aren't that way. I don't think they want to know who you are. It's too complicated for them or something. And if you wave and say, "Hello there, Mrs. Gabel," Mrs. Gabel will look up and smile kind of nervous like and wave back. And you can tell she's trying to figure out who you belong to, but she'd never dare ask. As you pass by, you can feel her wishing you'd never say hi to her again because she doesn't really want to know who you are and it bothers her when you make her try to figure it out.

So I knew who Mrs. Cranston was. She lived across the cul-de-sac from Prunella. And I could almost hear her thinking, "Well, what have we here?" as she peeked at us from behind a curtain.

But after Dad explained, she smiled at me and said, "Why not?"

So I had a job, and right away she wanted the yards done. Mr. Cranston was pretty nice. He got the mower out for me and showed me what he wanted done, and before you know it, I was pushing and pulling on that mower making the blades go *wack-wack-wack-wack-wack!* It was a fine sound, and their backyard had a lot of shade, so I didn't sweat as much as I could've.

Then I noticed Mrs. Cranston peeking out a top-story window, just keeping an eye on me. Well, that felt kind of funny—like I was getting *spied* on or something. But I kept on going, *wack-wack-wack-wack-wack!*, and before you know it, I thought I was done.

Mrs. Cranston didn't. When she saw me winding down, she tapped on the window and pointed. I'd missed a spot. So I pushed the mower over the spot she was tapping at—not that it looked like it had been missed—and then she did it again.

It would have been nice if she'd opened the window and talked to me, but I guess she didn't want to let the air-conditioning out, so she just tapped and pointed until I was ready to scream.

Finally Mr. Cranston came out with a big glass of lemonade and told me that Mrs. Cranston liked having her lawn done in two directions. I'd never heard of such a crazy thing, but I just smiled and thanked Mr. Cranston for the lemonade and got back to work mowing the other direction.

By the time I was done, there were about ten extra pieces of grass in the catcher and a big smile on Mrs. Cranston's face.

I put the mower away, and Mr. Cranston came out and paid me and said what a good worker I was and that he'd see me at the same time next week. I thanked him and took the money, and thought as I walked home that it had sounded like a lot more money before I'd started working.

But I wasn't going to let Jack know that. Ever since he'd gotten the paper route, he'd been taking out his strongbox and counting all his money right in front of me. Sometimes three times. Out loud.

Anyhow, when I got home, Jack was out front folding papers by himself. He tried to ignore me, but when he saw the money sticking out of my hand, he couldn't. "They gave you *that* for mowin' a yard?"

I just smiled and said, "Yup."

Jack looked at his mess of papers and then back

at me and said, "So are you going to fold papers or what?"

I was tired and didn't feel much like folding papers, so I asked, "Where's Allen?"

Jack scowled. "Watching TV."

Well, it wasn't too long after that that Jack told Allen he'd *pay* him to do the papers twice a week.

Delivering papers is kind of fun. You get out there on your bike and sometimes you make some amazing shots. I know, because Allen let me help him. He'd take the left side of the street and I'd take the right. And we already knew which houses liked their papers porched and which houses didn't care from all those times we'd pedaled around with Jack.

When we'd get back, Jack would see us and get all upset because we were done so soon. Then one time when we got back really early, he told Allen that he wouldn't get any money unless he did the collecting too.

It didn't take long to figure out why Jack hated collecting so much. Sometimes I'd go around with Allen, but I couldn't actually help him collect because the *Daily News* had this stupid rule about girls, and Jack was afraid if they found out he'd lose the job.

Anyhow, we'd go around one night and half the people weren't home or didn't answer the door because they saw us coming. Then we'd go around the next night and half the people said they didn't have the money and to come back later. So we'd come back later and they'd spend twenty minutes searching the house for their pocketbook and usually they'd come back with an "I'm sorry, come back tomorrow." Collecting's the worst. It takes forever.

After a while Allen was doing all the work, and Mom stepped in and said, "Whose paper route is this, anyway?" That's when it came out that Jack didn't want the job anymore. I guess he was just tired of folding papers and counting his money.

I also think he wanted my job, because every week when I'd come home from being tapped at by Mrs. Cranston, he'd act all grumpy and try to find out if I was planning to quit. I'd just smile like Mrs. Cranston was the nicest lady in the world to work for and set about counting the money in my strongbox. I never told him that Mrs. Cranston made me edge the lawn with hand cutters or that she wanted the mower scrubbed and dried before it went back in the garage. Or how she'd tap at me if I mowed too *fast*.

And I was getting to the point where I would've let Jack have the job, but one day Mrs. Cranston actually opened the window and told me that they were moving and there wouldn't be any more work for me. I tried not to smile too much, but there are some things that you just can't help.

So the only person with a job was Allen, and he was getting pretty sick of it. I mean delivering papers is something you have to do every day whether you feel like it or not, and by the time you go through all the trouble of getting money out of people, well, it takes up a lot of time.

And I guess that's why we started taking turns. Every other day I'd slap on a baseball cap and fling those papers all over the neighborhood. No one ever complained that a *girl* was delivering their papers. And when it came time to do the collecting, I would wear that cap right up to the doorstep and say, "Collecting." They knew what for, and were probably thinking so hard about how to get out of paying that they didn't even notice I was breaking the rules.

Sometimes they'd look at me funny, but most people didn't even notice or didn't dare ask. Think about it—"Aren't you a girl?" is a pretty risky thing to say to a kid, especially if they're not!

But one time this lady answered the door in her bathing suit and was mad at me for bothering her. She was having trouble keeping her stupid dog inside. It was yipping and snapping and in general acting a lot bigger than it was. I'm sure you've seen the type—small with a bow holding up its hair so it can see. Dogs like that always act like they're going to tear your foot off. Probably all they really want is a decent haircut and to get rid of that bow, but their owners don't seem to understand that.

Anyhow she scowled at me from behind this white lipstick and said, "You're a girl!"

I did my best to look insulted, but she just laughed and slammed the door in my face.

That shook me up. I was tired and thirsty, and that lady just ruined my day. So at the next house I took off my cap and said, "Hi. My name's Carolyn and I'm helping my brother collect for the paper."

And you're not going to believe what happened. The lady said, "Now isn't that the sweetest . . . Harold! Come here! I want you to see this!"

So her husband came to the door and she told him what I was doing and made him pay for the paper *and* give me a fifty-cent tip.

Well, that put a smile right back on my face.

And you can bet what's in your strongbox that I said the same thing at every house I went to. And you know what? I liked saying it. Made me feel like I didn't have to cover my hair with a hat, or try to talk a little different so I'd sound like a boy.

And that's when I started thinking that maybe it wasn't so stupid being a girl—that maybe what was stupid was the rules that went along with it.

SCHOOL

chapter 12
Getting Ready

You'd think I'd be used to the way it happens. I've been going to Bradbury Elementary since kindergarten, and it always feels the same, so you'd think I'd be prepared, but I never am.

Things start to quiet down. Even the Moyers' house doesn't have as much going on. It's not that there's nothing to do—you just don't feel like doing it. You just sit on the porch and wilt. Even the Freekos seem boring.

And even with everything so slowed down, it still always catches me off guard when September rolls around.

And when it does, boy! Everything happens all at once. Cars show up in the parking lot at Bradbury Elementary. The guy with the riding mower cruises around cutting grass that's already been cut quite nicely. Busses start going through that big bus lane—they don't have any kids in them, they just come to the school and sit there with their motors running for fifteen minutes and then leave.

Don't ask me why, it's just what they do.

And then one day you hear that the doors are posted with who's in what classroom. The whole neighborhood races over to see who they got for a teacher and if their best friend is in the same class or not.

Will and Allen got the same class, which made Allen pretty happy. Charlie and I got the same class, which I was glad to see, though I don't know why because he never talked to me much at school. He didn't talk to any girls at school, so it didn't hurt my feelings too much. I just thought it was dumb.

Every year, right after the doors at school are posted, Mary comes over wearing a brand-new outfit. She stands there on our front porch kind of turning from side to side and leaves a couple of bags of hand-me-downs for me to sort through and wash the smell out of.

Now, don't get me wrong. The clothes aren't *dirty*. They're washed and folded, but you can smell that they've been someone else's clothes right through all that soap and bleach.

Anyhow, I dump the bags out on the floor in my room, hoping that there's something I'll like. I go through everything and pull out the few things that

I might actually want to wear. And then, as I'm stuffing everything else back into the sacks, Mom shows up.

To my mom, everything is usable. I'll be standing there in this awful dress with yellow and green flowers and birds, and she'll say, "Hmmm. We could take it in here ... hem it to about there ... it'll be fine." Yeah, and I'll be looking like a walking pet store.

But there's no arguing with her. Before you know it, it's taken in and hemmed and I'll have to wear it to school every time she asks, "Why don't you ever wear that nice dress with the birds on it?" Telling her you hate it doesn't do a bit of good. Mom likes the word "nonsense" and uses it whenever I say how ugly something is.

After the doors at school get posted, you wind up spending a lot of time in your room. Parents somehow think that cleaning out your closet and drawers is going to make you do better in school. The trouble with that isn't so much straightening everything out, it's the pile of stuff you have left when you're *done* straightening everything out. A pile of stuff that doesn't actually belong anywhere.

When I was younger, Mom let me have a junk

drawer. Anything that didn't have a real place of its own wound up in the junk drawer. Nowadays she won't let me get away with that. So I work really hard at cleaning up, but I'm still always left with this pile of junk on the floor.

Probably most of it's stuff I could throw out and never miss. But it's neat stuff, or could be neat if only I'd fix it. Like this Pinocchio puppet I have. It's the kind with the strings hanging from a cross of wood, and you can make him walk and bend at the waist and wave. I used to have him hanging from the ceiling in my room until one day he fell and broke his nose. I was pretty upset and decided right away to glue his nose back on, but there was no glue in the whole stupid house. Well, maybe there was, but I couldn't find it. And I was afraid to ask my mom, because he fell when I accidentally hit him with a ball right after she'd yelled at me to quit bouncing it in the house.

So I hid Pinocchio in the closet along with his nose, and before you know it he was all tangled up and his nose was missing. I've looked real hard for that nose, but so far I haven't found it, and every year right before school starts, Pinocchio's right there in the middle of the pile, all tangled up and staring at me. I don't know what to do with him. I can't hang him back up with that hole in his face, but I would feel terrible throwing him out just because he has a little problem with his nose.

Eventually I take one last look around for his nose and then put him back in the closet and try to forget about him. About that time Mom comes in and stands there for a while, staring at the pile. Finally she sighs and helps me until it's all put away.

And after the closet and drawers are cleaned out and the pile's finally gone, there's no sense in even trying to get anyone to play with you. Everyone's too busy getting ready for school. At least that's what their mothers tell you when you knock on the door. I think it's more that the *moms* are getting ready for their kids to go to school, and the kids are in their rooms trying to decide what to do with a pile of stuff that would fit quite nicely into a certain bottom drawer if only they'd be allowed to put it there.

chapter 13
The Dragon Lady

When school finally does start, you're almost glad because you're so tired of getting ready that going to school almost sounds like fun.

Usually you know what a teacher's going to be like because someone you know has had them before. This year, though, I didn't know what to expect, because my name was posted on the door of this brand-new teacher—Mrs. Rennalds.

At first I thought Mrs. Rennalds wasn't going to be bad. She spoke real soft and was nice as can be. Then she caught David looking up Julie's dress.

At Bradbury Elementary the girls have to wear dresses, and I'm sure you can guess what I think of that. I mean, how are you supposed to play on the monkey bars or play kickball or do *anything* fun in a dress? Even jumping rope is dangerous in a dress.

Most of the girls don't seem to mind. Especially girls like Julie. Julie wears party dresses to school. Her mom does her hair up with ribbons, and she's got curls like a stupid doll. If my mom did that to me, you can bet I'd have the ribbons torn out before I crossed the street and I'd be wetting my hair down in the bathroom. Not Julie. She *likes* looking that way.

And I swear she has ten pairs of Mary Janes. The shiny kind. She has black ones with bows and black ones without, she's got white ones that never have any scuff marks on them, and then a red pair and even a *green* pair that she wore at last year's Christmas play. Who's ever heard of a green pair of Mary Janes?

So Julie's always dressed like she's going to some fancy party, and everyone's used to that, but this year she wore lipstick and *nylons* on the first day of school. Boy, did she get a lot of attention—especially from Helen Lison. I don't like Helen. She's always whispering about people and lying about things.

Julie doesn't wear nylons or lipstick anymore, so I think maybe Mrs. Rennalds had a talk with her, but she still wears those stupid party dresses. And they do kind of flip up when she sits down, so it's no wonder that David was trying to look up her dress that day.

If she'd been wearing shorts under her dress like

I always do, it wouldn't have been any big deal. Shorts let you do anything you want and not worry about your underwear showing. I don't know why all the girls don't wear them. Debbie and Gail are the only other ones who do, so as far as I'm concerned the rest of the girls are just plain dumb.

Anyway, the minute Mrs. Rennalds saw David looking up Julie's dress, our teacher with that soft, sweet voice turned into a monster. Scared the daylights out of all of us. She swooped down on David and grabbed him by the arm so hard he yelped. Then she got right in his face and hissed and snapped for a few minutes until he was just about crying. Then she yanked him up by the arm and dragged him out of the classroom, and we could hear her through the door hissing and snapping some more.

Well! We all looked around at each other, too scared to say anything. But when she came back in, she smiled real sweetly and said in that soft voice, "Now, class, get back to work," like nothing had happened.

Turns out David spent the rest of the morning waiting for the principal to punish him, but all Dr. Berrywine did was talk to him about his Little

League team. Then right before he left, he told him that he shouldn't look up girls' dresses.

After that we started noticing things about Mrs. Rennalds. For one thing, she likes to chew gum when she drinks her coffee. She keeps a coffee cup and a thermos on her desk next to the jar of pencils we're not allowed to borrow. And since *we're* not allowed to eat or drink in class or chew gum at all, this didn't seem fair to us.

I wouldn't have minded so much except she never washed the coffee cup. You'd go up to ask her a question and you couldn't help but stare at that cup, all black on the inside and smudgy red from lipstick on the outside.

And it's not just that she drinks coffee; she also eats cookies. She probably thinks we don't know about the cookies because she sneaks them, but she's always got chunks of chocolate stuck in her teeth and she's always sucking or picking at her teeth, trying to keep them clean. She keeps the cookies in one of her desk drawers, and you can hear her rolling the drawer back ever so quiet. If you look up through your bangs, you can see her check that no one's watching, and *pop* there goes a cookie, right in her mouth.

This is a good time to raise your hand and ask if you can go to the bathroom or out for a drink of water. She can't talk with that cookie jammed in her mouth, so she just smiles and nods and off you go.

As long as Mrs. Rennalds has her coffee and we stay pretty quiet, she's okay. At least until right before recess. If you're going to do something to make her mad, it's best to do it first thing in the morning. She doesn't seem to mind so much in the morning. But if you do it right before recess or lunch, boy, does the monster come out!

It takes a few weeks to figure out what a new teacher's like and when you can get away with what, but after a while you get the hang of her. Then you start wondering *why* she does what she does. At first I thought the monster came out because she was hungry, but that didn't make sense with all the cookies she goes through. Then Debbie told me it was because she needed a cigarette. Debbie says that her mom gets cranky just like Mrs. Rennalds if she needs a cigarette. And sure enough, I started noticing that after recess or lunch, you could smell that cigarette smell on her, right through her perfume.

So everyone started calling her Dragon Lady.

No one ever called her Mrs. Rennalds unless they were talking to her or to the principal. Mom and Dad wouldn't let me do it at home, so I called her "D.L." until they were so used to it, they didn't even think about what it stood for.

Usually I can do my work on my own, but sometimes I don't understand something and neither does anybody around me. So someone's got to go up and ask the Dragon Lady to explain it and then get permission to explain it to the other kids. Usually that person is me.

When you go up for help, she gets her face right up to yours and whispers because she doesn't want the class to be disturbed. And out of her mouth come words, but sometimes they don't quite make it into your brain because her coffee-gum-cigarette breath just about makes you gag. And her mouth does this funny twitching thing as she tries to move her gum out of the way, only it won't go because it's stuck on a tooth right there near the front of her mouth, all full of cookie crumbs, kind of stretching between her teeth like dirty green taffy.

After a while, no one even talked about her gum or the cookies anymore because everyone'd seen it and talked about it so much already. But what no one had ever noticed was that she wore a wig.

At first I wasn't sure. But as she bent forward to work out a math problem for me, I could see this little bald spot at the back of her head. Only it wasn't bald like my dad's head—it was bald like a rug. You could see this open weave where hair was supposed to be.

I must have been staring at it pretty good, because it took a while for her voice to register. "Carolyn . . . Carolyn!" she was saying.

I jumped and said, "Yes, ma'am?"

Well, the Dragon Lady came out fast. "You haven't heard a word I've been saying!"

I jumped back a little. The whole class was looking at me—even Charlie, which was real embarrassing.

"*Have* you?"

"I'm sorry, ma'am," I whispered, and peeked up at her as she tried to decide what to do with me. Finally she said, "Well, just sit down and figure it out for yourself then!"

I was so relieved. And when I got back to my seat, I leaned forward and whispered to Debbie in front of me, "D.L. wears a *wig*!"

Before you know it half the class was raising

their hands wanting to go up and get something explained, and she was helping them in groups, not knowing that they were pointing to her bald spot trying to keep from laughing.

By the time recess came around, everyone was so excited about the Dragon Lady's wig that we all ran around the blacktop telling everyone we knew, "Dragon Lady wears a wig! Hey! Have you heard? D.L. wears a wig!" I'm sure that by the end of recess, even the first graders knew about it.

And, it turns out, so did the principal.

chapter 14
What to Do With Miss McPew

Before I tell you what the principal did to me, I've got to explain: I never get in trouble at school. I get in trouble at home all the time, but I have two brothers and it's just something that happens when you're outnumbered like that. But at school I get good grades and I'm pretty quiet and teachers like me fine. No teacher's ever sent me to the principal's office. Well, there was the trouble I had with Miss McPew last year, but she wasn't really my teacher.

Miss McPew is in charge of the orchestra, and I've known her since the third grade. Every year I joined because my mom said I should and because you get out of class once a week. What I didn't like about orchestra—besides Miss McPew—was that none of my friends were in it. Debbie didn't play an instrument, Gail was only in band, and Charlie— well, Charlie liked baseball a lot better than music.

Playing flute wasn't that bad. All I really had to do was figure out how to blow into it. The string people had a lot more to worry about. They were always holding their bows wrong or something. And some of those things get pretty big! Poor Cathy Tunn had to carry her cello to school and back, and Miss McPew would yell at her over and over not to drag it on the ground. So the flute wasn't as bad as you might think.

Trombone would have been better, though. With trombone you don't really hit bad notes. You slide around until the right note comes along and then stay there until you have to go to the next note and then you just slide over to it. There's no sliding around on the flute. When you hit a bad note, everyone around you knows it and they look at you out of the corners of their eyes, wondering what in the world you're doing. I know, because I've done that myself with Penny Mercantile. Penny's first chair and has always been first chair except for the time I stared at her out of the corner of my eye while I was challenging her. It messed her up so bad, she blew it and I got to be first chair for a whole month.

Ever since then, anytime I hit a bad note, Penny Mercantile's eyes scoot over in her head, and she stares at me until she loses her place and has to look at the music again. I try to ignore her because it's my trick and I don't want her using it on me, but sometimes I get messed up so bad that I just pretend to play.

And that's how the trouble with Miss McPew started. She was always so busy yelling at the strings that she never noticed when I was faking it.

Then one day we were in the middle of some song when she tapped on the podium and hollered for everyone to be quiet. When everyone had finally squeaked to a stop, she turned to me and said, "We can't hear the flutes!"

Well, I wonder why. The flutes there that day were Sharon Zimmer and me, and Sharon Zimmer's only in the third grade and so small that you forget she's there at all. Besides, I think she was faking it too.

Anyhow, Miss McPew tapped on the podium and we all got ready to play, only I didn't know where in the world we were. I didn't even know what piece of *music* we were supposed to be playing. I faked like I was playing and looked over at Sharon Zimmer's music, trying to figure out where we were. The trouble was, what Sharon was playing sounded so terrible that I was sure she was looking at the wrong piece of music too. Maybe the

reason we all sounded so terrible was that nobody
knew what piece of music we were on, and everyone was playing something different.

So I was all caught up in thinking this when
Miss McPew hollered at us to stop again. Everyone jumped. Miss McPew is scary! She's short and
really fat and has eyes that go in different directions. On top of that she sprays all over you when
she yells.

She didn't yell at me this time, though. Instead
she slammed down her baton, walked over to
Cathy Tunn, and yanked that cello right out of her
hands. For a minute we all thought she was going
to hit her with the bow, but instead she pushed
Cathy out of her chair and sat down.

Playing the cello is hard to do gracefully if
you're a girl. You've got to spread your legs out and
pull the stupid thing up to you, and if you don't
watch out, your underwear shows. And if you're as
fat as Miss McPew and you sit on one of those
folding chairs and play the cello, it's amazing what
you show off. She was wearing these nylons that
snap onto straps, only the nylons couldn't make it
much past her knees. Fat was coming out *every-*
where.

But she didn't seem too worried about her underwear. She just sat there tapping a foot, running that bow back and forth across Cathy's cello, bobbing her head from side to side. When she was done, she looked at Cathy and said, "There. That's how it's done. Now do you think maybe you can do that?"

Cathy gulped and nodded, but you knew darned well that she wasn't going to be able to play it right. When Miss McPew got back up to the podium and tapped her little baton, Cathy burst into tears and ran out of the room.

Miss McPew just ignored her and flipped that baton around from left to right like she was swatting flies. Half of us were still staring at the door Cathy had run out of, so even if we did happen to have the right piece of music on our stands, we didn't know where we were supposed to be. We just sat there, faking it.

Then all of a sudden she banged the baton on her podium so hard, it sounded like it was going to break. Everyone jumped again, and Sharon Zimmer started hiccuping like mad, popping up and down in her chair like a jack-in-the-box. Miss McPew turned to me and shouted, "We still can't hear the flutes!"

I looked down at my music and nodded, but she walked over to me and said, "Maybe you can play it so we *all* can hear."

I nodded and mumbled something, expecting her to walk back to her podium, but she didn't. She squinted at me and shouted, "NOW!"

I gulped and whispered, "By myself?"

She looked at Sharon Zimmer, bobbing up and down in her chair, gasping for air, and said, "Yes, by yourself!"

I started playing softly because I was sure I had the wrong piece of music in front of me. But after a while she started nodding, and it dawned on me that I did have the right music, so I played a little louder. Pretty soon she stopped me and said, "Now play it that way with everyone else. Nice and loud!"

I was so relieved that I didn't notice how badly Sharon Zimmer was shaking until we were halfway through the song. I looked at her sideways and saw that she was crying, so I put down my flute and whispered, "Are you okay?"

She just looked at me with tears running down her face and hiccuped really loud. That was enough to make ol' McPewy bring the orchestra to a grinding stop again. She put her hands on her hips and said, "What *is* the problem?"

I thought poor Sharon was going to turn inside out with those hiccups, and she might have if the lunch bell hadn't rung just then. I tore my flute apart and stuffed it into the case without even drying it. And I was planning to grab my music and run, only poor Sharon Zimmer was hiccuping so bad, she couldn't take apart her flute. She finally let go of it and let me do it for her.

The whole time, Miss McPew was just picking up her music and pretending she didn't hear Sharon Zimmer turning inside out. When Sharon finally quit shaking enough to hiccup her way out the door, I looked over at Miss McPew and decided— I quit.

I didn't go up to her and say, "McPewy, I hate your guts and I quit," like I should have. I left school right in front of the lunch monitor, went home, and made a petition with big letters that said: WE QUIT UNTIL YOU'RE NICER!

Mom raised her eyebrows and scratched her cheek. "Are you sure you want to do this?"

So I told her about Cathy Tunn and Sharon Zimmer and everything, and she said it was fine if

I quit, but did I really want to do this? I was so mad that I said, "YES!" which made Mom smile this funny little smile and kiss me, of all things.

When I got back to school, I barely had enough time to show off the petition before the bell rang. And then nobody wanted to sign it. *Nobody*. I couldn't believe it. Then Jeff Rice told me that nobody wanted to sign it because nobody wanted to sign it *first*. I put my signature down and pretty soon the whole paper was full of names. What I didn't know was that the person who signed first was the one who would get in trouble.

The next time we had orchestra, only the people who were too chicken to sign the petition went to practice. Everybody else stayed in class. Everybody except me. I had to give the petition to Miss McPew.

When I got there, McPewy was looking around and you could tell—she was wondering where everyone was. I almost turned around, but instead I went up to her podium and put down the petition. Then I ran like mad to get out of there.

When I got back to class, I felt really, really good. That lasted until a messenger came to our classroom with a note that said I had to go straight to the principal's office.

Now, maybe you've been to the principal's office a bunch of times and think it's no big deal. Not me. I wasn't even sure where the principal's office *was*, and by the time I found it, I was thinking that maybe it wasn't such a hot idea, me putting that petition together.

Dr. Berrywine didn't say much at first. He sat back in his chair and played with a pencil—twirling it around, chewing on it, doodling with it. And while he was doodling, I was sitting on the edge of my chair, shaking about as bad as Sharon Zimmer. Finally he said, "I suppose you know why you're here."

Well, of course I did, but what came out of my mouth was "No, sir."

He bit his cheek and nodded and started playing with that stupid pencil again. Then I noticed that right there in front of him was my petition. He shoved it forward, real slow like, and said, "Did you have anything to do with this?"

There was my name, right next to the number one, getting me in trouble. So I studied my hands, shaking away in my lap, and just kind of nodded.

"Hmmm," he said.

Now, *Hmmm* can mean a lot of things, but when

a grown-up says it to you just right, it means you're in trouble. And after they say it, they just sit there and you know that what they're doing is deciding. Deciding exactly how they're going to punish you. And all you can do is sit there and wait for them to come up with something.

That's what Dr. Berrywine was doing, and he was taking the longest time doing it. Finally he leaned forward a little and said, "Miss McPew isn't that bad, is she?" I just sat there, looking at my hands. "Is she, Carolyn?"

I looked up at him, and he looked like he really did want to know, so I said, "Yes."

He laughed a little—not mean or anything—then sat back in his chair and picked up the petition and shook his head. "Tell me what she does that's so bad."

That caught me by surprise. I sat up a little and blinked a lot. "She's just mean."

"How is she mean?"

So I told him. At first I was whispering, but after I got going, boy! I told him about Sharon Zimmer's hiccups and *everything*. And he stayed real still and listened. When I finished, he just sat there, chewing on the side of his mouth.

Finally he looked at me and said, "Carolyn, why don't you give orchestra another try? I think you'll find that Miss McPew is really a very nice lady."

I stared at him for a minute. I wanted to say, "She is not!" but I stopped myself because I could tell he was going to let me go without yelling at me or standing me in a corner or doing any of the other things they say that principals do. Instead, I just stared at the pen-and-pencil set on his desk until he said, "What do you say, Carolyn?"

Well, what *could* I say? I nodded, and that was good enough for him. He stood up and said, "Why don't you get back to class now?"

So the next time we had orchestra practice, I went, and Miss McPew was sweet as pie to everyone. And just when we were starting to relax, thinking maybe orchestra wasn't so bad after all, Miss McPew made her way over to me.

I smiled at her and she smiled back at me. At least I thought it was a smile, so it scared the daylights out of me when she grabbed my ear and turned my head and whispered, "I'd better not get any more trouble from you, little girl!"

My ear was burning from her yanking on it, and I looked up sideways as best I could. There she was with that smile on her face, looking like she was going to kill me.

She finally let go of my ear, and I rubbed it and watched her go back to her podium like nothing had happened. Everyone started playing. Everyone but me. I was watching her and realizing that she was just as mean as ever and I got mad. Really, really mad. I took my flute apart, threw it in the case, and left. Just like that.

And I never went back. Dr. Berrywine never said another word about it, and I pretty much stayed out of trouble after that.

Until the business of the Dragon Lady's wig came up.

chapter 15
Back to the Principal's Office

I don't know how they traced it back to me. Someone must've told on me, and I bet it was Helen, because she's always tattling on people. She probably marched right up to the principal's office and said, "Excuse me, Dr. Berrywine? Carolyn's making fun of Mrs. Rennalds' wig, and I think you should stop her."

This time when the messenger came, the note said that I had to go to the office. It didn't say anything about the principal. That happens sometimes when you forget something and your mom brings it to school for you, so on my way to the office I was trying to figure out what I could have forgotten. I couldn't think of anything, and even if I had forgotten something, I didn't think Mom would've noticed, because she was getting kind of close to having the baby and was pretty distracted.

I'd actually forgotten about the Dragon Lady's wig until I got to the office and was told Dr. Berrywine wanted to see me.

If a principal was really smart, he'd call kids into his office to tell them what a good job they were doing, or to congratulate them on their grades, or for winning a race or something. If principals did that, they'd keep you guessing.

But principals don't do that, and the minute I found out Dr. Berrywine wanted to see me in his office, I knew I wouldn't be leaving with any ribbons. So into his office I went, and the funniest thing happened. I sat down in the same chair I'd sat in before, and Dr. Berrywine looked the same as he had when McPewy got me in trouble, so my hands *should've* been shaking, but they weren't. I just sat there and looked at him.

He gave me a little smile and said, "Hello, Carolyn."

I swung my legs a little and smiled back and said, "Hi." Just like that, "Hi."

He said, "How are you?" and actually I was feeling okay, though I didn't really know why. I mean, I was in trouble, there was no doubt about it, and here I was swinging my legs, feeling fine. So I said, "Fine, thank you."

He kind of chuckled to himself and said, "Do you know why you're here?"

I opened my eyes real big and said, "Not exactly, sir."

He played with his pencil a minute while I just sat there looking at him. Finally, he said, "Does your mother have a wig?"

Well, my mouth just kind of took over. "Yes, sir, but she never wears it. She says it's hot and makes her head itch and I'm glad, because it looks pretty funny on her anyway." My legs were pumping away, having a good old time.

Dr. Berrywine bit the side of his cheek. "It does, does it?"

I nodded and said, "Besides, it's kind of red."

Dr. Berrywine didn't have much to say to that. He just sighed and said real quiet, "Carolyn, it's not nice to make fun of people the way you've been making fun of Mrs. Rennalds today."

I looked down and said, "We weren't making fun of her. We just didn't know until today."

"You don't think calling someone 'Dragon Lady' and 'Carpet Head' is making fun of them?"

Well, Dragon Lady I'd called her a million times, but Carpet Head? Boy! That was a good one! It took everything I had not to bust up right there. I opened my eyes real big and said, "Carpet Head? I've never called her Carpet Head."

He looked at me the way Mom does when all the cookies have disappeared from the cupboard. "Oh?"

"No sir!"

"I see. Well, maybe you could spread the word that if I hear of anyone calling Mrs. Rennalds Dragon Lady or Carpet Head, they'll be in to see me after school."

"Yes, sir."

He stood up, so I stood up too. "Carolyn, Mrs. Rennalds doesn't know why you were called to the office, and I'd like it to stay that way. It's hard being a new teacher, and I'd appreciate it a lot if you could help make her feel welcome here."

That caught me off guard, him asking me to help him out. So I looked at him and nodded and told him I would try.

On my way back to class I didn't run, I didn't even walk fast. I stopped and had a long drink of water at the water fountain and wondered if Dr. Berrywine's wife ever wore a wig.

chapter 16
Roy G. Biv

Some teachers are fun to answer questions for. Take Miss Emigh back in fourth grade—when she'd ask a question, I'd raise my hand whether I was sure of the answer or not. Whenever I got the answer right, she'd say, "Wonderful!" or "Very good, Carolyn!" And if I didn't get the answer right, she'd find something right about it anyway and say, "Thanks for contributing, Carolyn," and call on somebody else.

Answering questions for Mrs. Rennalds is not fun. If you get the answer right, she'll give you a little smile and say, "That's right," but she'll always find something else to add to your answer, so you wind up feeling like you didn't really get it right at all.

And if you get the answer wrong, she gives you a little frown and says, "Hmmm," and then, "Anyone else?"

So I don't raise my hand much in Mrs. Rennalds' class, and I never volunteer things without being called on. But one day during art she was writing the colors of the rainbow on the chalkboard, explaining about their order and how we should memorize them because they'd be on a test later that week.

My dad taught me the colors of the rainbow a long time ago, and I've never forgotten them because of Roy G. Biv. That's not a person—it's the first letter of the colors of the rainbow broken up into a name. You know—Red, Orange, Yellow, Green, Blue, Indigo, Violet.

So I raised my hand. And I held it up for a long time. When she finally noticed it, she was in the middle of talking about indigo and interrupted herself to say, "What is it, Carolyn?"

I said, "My dad taught me a way to—" and that's as far as I got.

"Carolyn, I'm in the middle of an explanation! I'm sure your father is a very smart man, but please, listen to what I have to say!"

When we finally got to work on our art project, I told Debbie and Gail about Roy G. Biv. They thought it was a great way to remember the colors of the rainbow, and wound up telling some other kids.

Mrs. Rennalds never did ask me what I was trying to tell her. And after school while Allen and I were riding our bikes to our piano lessons, I realized that the reason she didn't ask was because I was just a kid. She figured I didn't know anything she didn't already know. Anything important, anyway.

Then Allen said, "Race you!" and I forgot all about Mrs. Rennalds and Roy G. Biv and concentrated on catching up with Allen. Our piano teacher, Miss Melby, lives way down Lemon Street, and Allen had never beat me there. Even when he had a head start, I always caught him.

I don't mind piano lessons because Miss Melby's nothing like Miss McPew—she's a real nice lady. She wears pointy glasses with sparkly little designs on them and dresses that are always busting with flowers. But the thing about Miss Melby that makes you keep watching her from the corner of your eye is that she sweats more than any lady you've ever seen.

While you're in the middle of your lesson, she sits on a stool by the piano bench, blotting away. It comes streaming down around her hair and down her neck, and if she doesn't keep moving that hanky, pretty soon it's dripping all over the piano keys. She doesn't give piano lessons during the summer, and it's probably because she'd float away.

I get my lesson first while Allen sits in this big puffy chair in Miss Melby's waiting room, and then he goes while I sit.

You can hear the piano from the waiting room, but you can't tell what Miss Melby's saying unless you sneak up the hall and listen. I've done that a couple times, but pretty much all she says is "Coming along . . . coming along," just like she does with me.

Anyhow, I was sitting in the puffy chair, waiting, when Miss Melby poked her head in and said, "Carolyn, come here a moment. I'd like you to hear this."

I followed her, and there was Allen looking pretty proud of himself. Miss Melby said, "Go ahead, Allen," and his fingers started flying around, playing one of the songs out of *my* book. He hit hardly any bad notes, and when he got done I stared. "When did you learn to play that?"

He just smiled. "I've been practicing!"

Now, as far as I knew, Allen never practiced. I knew he went down to little Andy's and banged on their piano in the garage, but I figured he was just messing around. But after hearing Allen play one of *my* songs, I knew something was going on down in little Andy's garage besides "Chopsticks."

And I was just thinking that I'd better start practicing a little harder if I was going to stay ahead of Allen when Miss Melby said, "I think maybe we should have a little contest next week. Perhaps on identifying notes? Allen, you're still having a bit of trouble with that—maybe this will make you study them." She turned to me, "What do you say, Carolyn? Are you game?"

Well, that caught me off guard. I mean, Miss Melby's not the kind of lady to have contests. You come in, play, hear "Coming along . . . coming along" a few times, get your assignment, and leave. But Allen asked, real excited, "Is there going to be a prize?"

Miss Melby laughed. "Sure, we can have a prize." She thought a minute. "How about a rubber lizard?" And then she pulled this huge rubber lizard out of the piano bench. "This little fellow."

Allen's eyes bugged out, and mine must have too, because Miss Melby laughed, then blotted some sweat. "So you practice, Allen, and if you know your notes better than Carolyn, this little fellow will be yours."

Normally I wouldn't have been worried about winning the contest. I know my notes pretty well. And I would've been sure I knew them better than Allen except for the fact that he knew how to play one of my songs. If he knew that, maybe he also knew his notes.

There are two sets of notes: EGBDF for the notes on the lines and FACE for the notes in the spaces. FACE is easy to remember, but with the notes on the lines I have a little more trouble.

So every day after school I'd practice my lesson and then I'd practice my notes. I don't know if it was that I wanted the lizard so much or if I just didn't want Allen to beat me.

After about the third day of practicing, Allen came in, sat next to me on the bench, and said, "Eebie geebie back da freezie."

I looked at him like he was nuts. "What do you want?"

"Eebie geebie back da freezie."

"Leave me alone, would you? I'm in the middle of practicing." I figured he was just trying to wreck my concentration.

He finally left, and I spent a few more minutes pretending to practice, but I was really thinking, "Eebie geebie back da freezie? How stupid can you get?"

When our next piano lesson rolled around, Allen and I got on our bikes and raced to Miss Melby's. I had my lesson, he had his, and when it was finally time for the contest, Miss Melby sat us both down on the bench. "Are you ready?"

She put up a piece of sheet music that neither of us had ever seen before and pointed to a note. In my mind I'm going, "E-G-B..." really fast, but before I could say the note, Allen said, "D!" I couldn't believe it. Then it happened again, and again. I got some of them faster than him, but by the time it was all over, he was jumping up and down waving the lizard around and I was standing there, wanting to cry.

Miss Melby said, "Excellent job, Allen! You too, Carolyn, but Allen has really improved!" Then she asked, "What did you do to study?"

Allen pointed to the sheet music and went up the staff saying, "Eebie Geebie Back Da Freezie."

I stared at the music and was thinking, "Eebie Geebie Back Da Freezie . . . EGBDF!" when Miss Melby laughed and said, "Every Good Boy Deserves Fudge didn't work for you?"

We both stared at her a minute, and finally she said, "Didn't I teach you that? I teach all my students that."

"You didn't teach *us* that!"

She just laughed and blotted. "Looks like Allen figured it out for himself."

When we were outside unlocking our bikes, I thought about how I'd told Allen to get lost when he interrupted my practicing with Eebie Geebie Back Da Freezie. It never even occurred to me that it might mean something.

Then I remembered how mad I got at Mrs. Rennalds about Roy G. Biv. And I was standing on Miss Melby's walkway feeling really stupid for not thinking I could learn anything from Allen when I heard, "Race you!"

I looked down the street and knew—this time I wouldn't be able to catch him. I was already way too far behind.

chapter 17
Smack, Squiggle Squiggle!

Helen Lison is a tattletale and I don't like her. She's also the biggest show-off in the world. Whenever we have to get up in front of the class and give a report, or even if we just have to work a problem at the board or be in a spelling bee, Helen Lison does her little squiggle thing.

She'll be spelling a word like *chocolate*, and she'll put her hands behind her back and bounce up and down and move from side to side. And she gets this look on her face like she's so smart, which she's not. Then her mouth smacks together and makes this sound that most kids only make when they're sucking on a milk shake.

Smack, squiggle squiggle, "C!" *smack*, squiggle squiggle, "H!" *smack*, squiggle squiggle, "O!" *smack*, squiggle squiggle, "C!" *smack* . . . And then she forgets where she is and has to start all over again. It just about drives me nuts. She never gets it right, even if it's a short word, and when the teacher tells her, "Sorry, Helen," she giggles and squiggles her way back to her seat.

I've been in the same class as Helen since the first grade, and it really gets to you after a while.

Every year Helen signs up for the talent show. Well, I do too, but that's only because my mom makes me. I hate it. I get all shaky and nervous, and I never win. I usually play the piano, which is what half the kids wind up doing. When you sit down at the piano, you can almost feel the audience yawning and thinking, "I wonder what's after this."

I'm not just imagining this, though that's what my mom thinks. Every year she comes to watch. Every year she tells me how proud she is of me. And every year all the kids who play piano lose.

Last year two sixth graders got up wearing torn-up old jeans and T-shirts and sweat bands, and they played electric guitars and shouted into the microphone so you couldn't understand what they were saying. And their guitars were so loud that all the mothers put their hands over their ears and shouted, "What?" back and forth to each other like a bunch of old people.

When they finished, one of the guys said, "We wrote that song ourselves."

And then the other guy said, "It took us ten minutes." Then they walked offstage and everyone clapped.

I think Dr. Berrywine was the one who liked them so much, because he clapped and clapped and clapped. Then he announced *me* and I had to do my piano piece, which I don't think anyone even heard because their ears were still ringing from those electric guitars.

Then came Helen with the same stupid act she does every year. Helen twirls a baton. She wore this white cowgirl outfit with fringe everywhere and a red tie and red boots. And she dropped the baton about ten times and giggled every single time. And when she was done, she took this grand bow and blew kisses to the judges. Can you believe it? I just hate Helen Lison.

After Helen was done dropping her baton and blowing kisses, the judges announced that the winner was the guys with the electric guitars. All the mothers shook their heads and all the kids who'd played piano swore they'd never play piano again. And Helen Lison played with the fringe on her outfit and giggled.

One night in October Mom shooed us out of the house because she had a headache and we wouldn't quit making noise. Jack went over to Billy's and Allen went over to Will's. I didn't know what to do—nothing seemed fun, especially by myself. So I climbed up into the tree house and just sat there for a while.

And that's when Charlie came over. Charlie hardly ever comes over, and if he does, it's because his mom needs to borrow something from my mom or he's selling candy bars for Little League. He never comes over to play with me.

So I watched him from the tree house. He walked clear around on the sidewalk instead of cutting across the grass, and then he walked up to the front door and stood there awhile. I decided to say hi, and he smiled and waved, and before you know it he was up in the tree house with me.

It was kind of weird, but I liked it. I don't think Charlie had ever been up in the tree house. Not with me, anyway. Anytime I played with Charlie, it was at his house or down the cul-de-sac if he wanted me to field grounders for him. Everyone always went over to the Moyers'. It was like head-quarters or something.

But there was Charlie, in the tree house, just talking about stuff. And I was still trying to figure out what he was doing there when he asked, "What do you think of Helen?"

I blinked. "Helen? Helen *Lison*?"

He looked out between the slats of the tree house and nodded.

"I *hate* her!" I said.

He was still looking between some boards, at what I don't know. Finally he asked, "How come?"

So I told him. About her stupid cowgirl outfit and how she giggles all the time and about the way she acts when she's in a spelling bee and everything else. I was getting really carried away, telling him how stupid Helen Lison was, when all of a sudden I had this terrible thought. "You don't *like* her, do you?"

He shrugged. "No, I was just wondering."

That made me feel a little better, so I talked about her some more, and then all of a sudden we didn't seem to have anything to talk about and Charlie left. I watched him walk down the sidewalk and around the corner, and I felt kind of funny. Like I shouldn't have been so mean about Helen Lison.

Then I remembered how she blows kisses, and I decided that I should have pointed *that* out to Charlie, too.

The next day Debbie came racing up to me at recess. "Did you hear?"

"Hear what?"

"About Charlie and Helen."

"What about them?"

"They're going steady!"

I just stood there and stared at her until she said, "Carolyn?"

I kept right on staring, which is not something I usually do. I mean, when Debbie told me that Darrell had asked Julie to go steady because he liked her *feet*, did I stand there and stare? No. Did I say, "*What?*" and blink like an idiot? No! I said, "Boy, is he dumb!" like anyone would.

But there I was, staring at Debbie, blinking like I couldn't see right. "*What?*"

And Debbie said it again, "Charlie and Helen are going steady!"

I don't know what came over me. I could tell I was going to start crying any minute, and that made me mad. So I stared some more and said, "Are you *sure?*"

Debbie rolled her eyes. "Of course I'm sure. She showed me his St. Christopher!"

"His St. Christopher?"

"Yeah, she's wearing it around her neck. Go ask her!"

Well, I didn't need to ask her. She was showing

it off to everyone, and squiggling and giggling and just being Helen. I wanted to punch her.

For the rest of school I didn't talk to anyone. I hid in the bathroom because I was going to cry any minute, and then everyone would be whispering, and who knew what stupid things they'd say! Like I had a crush on Charlie or something dumb like that. And sitting in the bathroom thinking about it made me even madder. Why in the world would Charlie want to go steady with *Helen*? He knew she squiggled and giggled and was the world's biggest show-off. He probably even knew about the way she blew kisses.

And Helen would never play kickball in his backyard. She'd probably show up in a *dress* or her cowgirl outfit and just watch and squiggle the whole time. And there's no way Helen would ever play in underground forts or field grounders in the street. So what good was she?

I sat there in the stall, swinging my legs back and forth, looking at the scabs on my knees from when I tripped playing hide-and-seek. It suddenly hit me that Helen probably had perfect little knees with no scars or scabs anywhere. Helen probably didn't even *own* a pair of shorts she could wear under a dress, and Helen probably had a room full of dolls and curtains of lace.

And Helen Lison had probably never wished she was a boy.

It turned out that Charlie and Helen went steady for four days. Now, I didn't know it was only going to be four days, so it seemed like a long time to me. That doesn't mean I was stupid about it or anything. I went to school and acted pretty normal. I even tried to be nice to Helen, which would've been easier if she'd quit twirling that St. Christopher for thirty seconds.

And when I said hi to Charlie, I tried to act like nothing had happened, but that wasn't easy either. I was feeling really dumb for having told him what an idiot I thought Helen was. I wanted to say I was sorry, but I wasn't sorry, which is a confusing way to feel.

Then one day I was walking home from school and heard, "Hey, Carolyn! Carolyn, wait up!"

I was in the middle of crossing the street, but I turned around anyway, and when I saw it was Charlie, I stopped. Just like that. In the middle of the street. I stopped and waited for him to catch up.

When he did catch up, he didn't say much of anything. We got to the corner where my house is and I had to go one way and he had to go the other. So we just stood there, looking at the sidewalk. And it hit me that we weren't acting like we'd known each other since before kindergarten. We were acting like we had when we first met.

I don't remember leaving our old house and moving into this house. The first thing I remember about moving was standing on the corner with my mom, meeting Charlie. I don't think I said much of anything. I just hid behind my mom and peeked out every now and then at Charlie peeking at me from behind *his* mom. I remember Mrs. Moyer and my mom talking and laughing, and I remember spending a lot of time staring at the cracks in the sidewalk.

I don't think I'd noticed the cracks since then, and now suddenly there they were, hypnotizing me. I couldn't do anything but stare at them and wish my mom and Mrs. Moyer were there so we'd have something to hide behind.

Finally, Charlie said, "Helen and I broke up."

Well, that made me look right up from those cracks. "You *did?*"

He nodded and started digging in his pocket. "I guess you were right."

I didn't say anything, but I was thinking that it was about time he got some brains about Helen Lison. Then he pulled his St. Christopher out of his pocket and kind of held it up and straightened it out right there in front of me. And for a second my heart started going really fast because I thought he was going to give it to me. I watched it twist and sparkle in front of me, and I was thinking that it was the most beautiful color blue I'd ever seen. Then he put it over his head and smiled.

Well, what was I supposed to do? I smiled back and tried to ignore that my heart had just about beat out of my chest when I thought he was going to put the chain around *my* neck. And it made me mad at myself, because I don't *want* my heart to do that around Charlie, and lately it's been doing it more and more.

Then Charlie laughed, like all of a sudden he felt real good. He said, "See you later!" and ran home.

I stood there on the corner watching him as he popped into his side gate, and after I stared at that gate for a while, I sat down on the curb and stared at the cracks some more. I just sat there and stared and wondered what the first thing Charlie remembers is.

It doesn't seem fair that it probably doesn't have a thing to do with me.

chapter 18
The Christmas Choir

I wish I could say that Mrs. Rennalds quit wearing that wig and that the Dragon Lady never came out again, but it wouldn't be true. What happened was we all got used to her. She still drank coffee and smoked and chewed gum with cookie crumbs in it, and that bald spot on her head seemed to get bigger every time you looked for it. But after Dr. Berrywine called me to his office, I quit calling her D.L. or Dragon Lady, and even though some kids still called her Carpet Head, most of us just called her Mrs. Rennalds.

And the day she told Helen Lison to quit giggling, I actually started to like her.

We all had to give reports on what our mom or dad did for a living. When it was Helen's turn, she was up there squiggling and giggling, and after about five minutes of her not getting anywhere with her report, Mrs. Rennalds said, "Helen! Stop that incessant giggling!"

I didn't exactly know what incessant meant, but

I figured it out pretty quick. Helen did stop giggling for about ten seconds, but she started up again, so Mrs. Rennalds sighed and said, "Helen, sit down!" and that's when I started liking Mrs. Rennalds.

I also like her because she's so excited about choir. Every year Bradbury Elementary puts on a Winter Pageant, and a big part of the show is the choir. People in the choir get to wear neat purple robes that go way down to your feet. Only the sixth graders can be in the choir. The fourth and fifth graders are in the Christmas play, and everybody else just has to watch.

I didn't like being in the play because there are too many kids and not enough parts, so most kids wind up just working backstage. And if you do get to be a cow or shepherd or something, you wind up wearing a costume that makes you sweat and you don't do much but go *moo* or *baa* every now and then.

Being in the choir is better than being in the play because you're almost always doing something. What I don't like is being told I'm a soprano when I know I'm not, or having to sing a harmony part when I'm standing right next to the alto section. It messes me up and I wind up singing the wrong part.

And I don't want to fake it. I like to sing.

Anyhow, Mrs. Rennalds was in charge of the choir, and you could tell she really liked doing it. She'd work with all the different sections and try like mad to teach us our parts. When all three sections would get something right, she'd jump up and down and say, "Yes! Very good! Wonderful!" And if we didn't get it, she'd just try over again. The Dragon Lady never came to choir practice.

And Mrs. Rennalds could *sing*. That really surprised me, because when you think about Mrs. Rennalds' mouth, you don't think music, you think coffee and cookies and sticky green gum. But she knew all the parts, and it really helped to have her sing along with us. She'd sing one part and then she'd switch over to another without hitting one wrong note. There's no way you can fake that.

So we practiced and practiced and practiced. And when the night finally came to do it for real, Mom surprised me with a new dress and some shoes. It seems stupid, but I got real excited, because Mom had never bought me a dress like *that* before. It wasn't full of bows and lace or anything, it was just a white dress with a couple of tiny reindeer on the collar, and I thought it was the best.

Only trouble was I couldn't wear my shorts. Mom said you could see them right through the dress even after I put on a slip, so I had to take them off.

Mom was running behind because I actually gave in and let her curl my hair a little. And Dad was running behind because he was having trouble convincing Jack to go see us in the Winter Pageant. Jack said that he had hated being in the choir when he was in the sixth grade, and that they did the same play every year and it was the boringest thing in the world. And you should've heard the way he said it. Like it was such a long time ago that he was in the sixth grade or something. And when I said, "Nuh-uh! You liked being in the choir! Besides, Allen's one of the *kings*," he looked at me like I was a stupid kid.

So Allen and I headed over to the school by ourselves, and right away Allen started looking for Will. Will wasn't hard to find, because he was sitting with his parents and Charlie in the same place they always sit, which is right next to where my parents always sit. Will seemed real happy to see Allen, and the two of them raced off to get into their costumes, which left me standing there feeling kind of uncomfortable.

Mrs. Moyer looked at me and sort of backed

away a little and said, "Why, Carolyn! Don't you look pretty tonight!"

That made me blush pretty good, because she was looking at me like she'd never seen me before. I thanked her real polite like, but she didn't leave it at that. She reached over and shook Mr. Moyer's arm. "Bob, doesn't Carolyn look lovely tonight?"

He glanced at me and said, "Mm-hmm."

I wanted to get out of there, but I didn't know where to go. It was too early to get into our robes, so I just stood there and blushed, looking at everything but Charlie. Finally Mrs. Moyer said, "Are your parents coming tonight?"

Okay. That gave me something to talk about. So I told her about Jack not being ready, but that sure, they were coming.

"Good, we'll save a couple of chairs for them."

I finally looked at Charlie out of the corner of my eye, and he was looking right at me. I blushed all over again and wished for a pair of shorts so I could at least go out and play. Instead I excused myself and started walking around like I had someplace to go.

When Mrs. Rennalds finally called that it was time for the choir to get ready, we all put on our robes and lined up on the bleachers. And before

you know it, it was time for us to start singing.
That's when Julie decided she should be standing
where I was standing so she could be next to
Darrell. Mrs. Rennalds' hands were up above her
head just twitching to start scooping and cutting air,
when Julie started whispering to me. I tried to
ignore her and watch Mrs. Rennalds, because I
didn't want to mess up, but Julie started tugging on
my robe and whispering really loud, "Switch with
me! Switch with me!" She'd already moved over
about three places, and I suppose I could've just
switched with her, but I didn't want to. Not
because I didn't want to ever, just not right then.
I was concentrating on Mrs. Rennalds' hands, trying to remember what I was supposed to do.

The whole cafeteria was really quiet because
they knew we were about to start, and that's when
Julie started pulling on me. Not just tugging on my
sleeve. *Pulling* on me until it felt like my new shoes
were going to slip out from underneath me and I
was going to fall off the bleachers and show
everyone my underwear.

I turned to her and said, "Stop it!"

And she said, "Switch with me! Switch with
me!" like a record that needs you to stomp on the
floor so it'll keep going.

So I hit her in the arm. Not hard or anything, just enough to get her to quit bugging me.

Julie must not have any brothers, though, because she thought it was real hard and started crying right there on the spot. She crinkled up and just *bawled*.

All of a sudden everyone in the cafeteria was trying to look around the heads in front of them to see what was going on, and the other kids were wobbling on the bleachers trying to get a better view. Mrs. Rennalds' hands quivered because she didn't know whether to start scooping and slashing or stop and find out what was going on in the soprano section.

Julie finally quit bawling, and what did she do? She looked at me and said, "Switch with me!"

I really wanted a bucket of water to pour over those stupid curls of hers. But I switched with her, and while I was doing it, I stomped on one of her stupid Mary Janes. She didn't seem to care, though; she just stood there, holding hands with Darrell.

Before you know it Mrs. Rennalds' hands scooped down and we were off and singing, turning pages and trying to get it just right. After a couple of songs I looked around for Mom and Dad and Jack, but when I finally spotted the Moyers, my parents weren't with them. And I could see empty seats next to the Moyers just waiting to get filled up.

That threw me off and I lost my place in the music. I wasn't about to look over at Julie's, so I just flipped the music back and forth, trying to find the spot with one eye and Mom and Dad with the other.

Mom and Dad always come to see us in plays and stuff, and I figured they had to be somewhere, so I sang on my tiptoes, twisting and turning, trying to find them.

It wasn't until after "Jingle Bells" that it hit me where they must be.

chapter 19
Nancy

I'd never really thought this through, and I don't think Allen or Jack had either. So when it happened, it jumbled up my feelings, and I know Allen and Jack were feeling peculiar, too.

Mom and Dad had told us not to talk about it too much. I think they wanted to make sure everything turned out all right and didn't want people asking them a bunch of silly questions.

I'd heard Mom answer, "It doesn't matter, as long as it's healthy," when people asked her whether she wanted a boy or a girl. And I heard that same answer over and over again, so I figured that it was the right answer.

But when Dad told me the baby was a girl, I started bawling my eyes out. It took me a long time to figure out I was crying because I was so happy. Happier than I'd ever been.

If anyone had asked me if I wanted the baby to be a boy or a girl and I'd stopped to think of my own answer, I don't know what I would've said.

There are two ways you can look at that question. First, did I want it to be a boy or a girl because it's better to *be* one or the other and what would I want for the baby's sake?

The other way of looking at it is what do *I* want it to be, which isn't really fair to the baby. But sitting there bawling, I realized that I wanted a sister more than anything in the world. Think about it— I've already got two brothers. You know how Jack is. And don't tell Allen, but he's going to be able to beat *me* up pretty soon. Besides, even though Allen and I play together a lot and you'd think he'd be on my side most of the time, he's not. Jack can be mean to him for weeks, and all he has to do is be nice for about thirty seconds and *whoosh!*, there goes Allen, over to his side.

And you get to an age when you don't want to go running to your mom just to have someone on your side. So you sit in your room wishing you were a boy so your brothers wouldn't do that to you. I never once thought that one of *them* should be a girl.

When Mom and Dad first brought Nancy home, we weren't allowed to breathe on her, let alone hold her. Mom was worried about us dropping her or hurting the soft spot on the top of her head, so mostly we got to watch Mom rocking her and feeding her. And since Nancy spent a lot of time sleeping, we had to do a lot of tiptoeing and whispering, which Jack and Allen didn't like too much.

I didn't mind, though. They'd go off and play, and sometimes they'd even invite me along, but most of the time I'd stay inside and watch Nancy sleep. You may not think that's too exciting, but she had the tiniest little fingernails and the most amazing little ears, and I didn't want to run around the neighborhood—I wanted to watch Nancy.

Then one day while Nancy was taking a nap, Mom asked me if I'd mind keeping an eye on her while she took a shower. I said, "Sure!" and about two minutes after Mom got in the shower, Nancy woke up crying.

I tried shaking a rattle, and I tried saying, "Sssh, sssh! Don't cry, Mom'll be right here," but that didn't work. So very carefully I reached into the crib and picked her up.

Then I sat down in the rocking chair and put her in the crook of my arm. And as we went back and forth, I sang her a little lullaby, and in no time she was quieting down. And as I looked at her and she looked at me, I knew—I wasn't going to be lonely anymore. I had a sister.

After a while Mom and Dad asked if we'd mind having the girls share one room and the boys share the other. I thought that was a great idea, and so did Allen. Trouble was Jack. He didn't want to share a room with Allen again and wound up talking Dad into letting him sleep in the garage.

So Jack moved his bed and dresser out there and then hung these bedspreads from the rafters for walls. I thought it was the greatest fort ever, but I didn't tell Jack that. I just told him the spiders were going to come back and get him.

So Allen's got Jack's old room and Nancy's crib is in mine. At night I look at her sleeping in the crib and I talk to her. I tell her about all the stuff that happened before she was born, just to catch her up. And I tell her what to look out for, being a girl. How being a girl is actually all right once you figure out that you should break some of the rules instead of just living with them.

I also tell her about the things I'm going to teach her the minute she's big enough—like touching the moon and spying and why you should stay away from ivy and girls who wear too much lace.

Now, you may think that's silly, talking to someone who's too little to understand and who's sleeping, but we learned in science that your brain stores away stuff it hears when you're asleep. If that's so, she's going to be pretty darned smart in no time at all.

And if you don't believe in stuff like that, I have proof that I'd tell you all about, only I'm thinking maybe I'll head over to the Moyers'. Allen said they were roasting hot dogs, and he said that Will said *Charlie* said I could come over if I wanted to, so I think maybe I will.

I like hot dogs. I like them a lot. And I'm thinking maybe Charlie's saving me a chair.

Wendelin Van Draanen is the best-selling author of the Sammy Keyes series. She grew up in Monrovia, California, where she spied on her neighbors, threw rocks down chimneys, and learned about touching the moon.